Mrs. (Matilda Charlotte) Houstoun

The way she won him

Vol. II

Mrs. (Matilda Charlotte) Houstoun

The way she won him
Vol. II

ISBN/EAN: 9783337052980

Printed in Europe, USA, Canada, Australia, Japan

Cover: Foto ©Andreas Hilbeck / pixelio.de

More available books at **www.hansebooks.com**

THE WAY SHE WON HIM.

A NOVEL.

BY

Mrs HOUSTOUN,

AUTHOR OF

"RECOMMENDED TO MERCY," "BARBARA'S WARNING,"
"SINK OR SWIM," "A HEART ON FIRE,"
ETC., ETC.

"On her *soul*, the fire had no power, nor was an hair of *her*
head singed, nor had the smell of fire passed on *her*."--
DANIEL IV. 27.

IN TWO VOLUMES.

VOL. II.

LONDON:

F. V. WHITE & CO.,
31 SOUTHAMPTON STREET, STRAND, W.C.

1891.

EDINBURGH
COLSTON AND COMPANY
PRINTERS

CONTENTS.

———o———

CHAPTER I.

Contents.

CHAPTER IX.

CHAPTER X.

CHAPTER XI.

CHAPTER XII.

CHAPTER XIII.

CHAPTER XIV.

CONCLUSION.

THE WAY SHE WON HIM.

NEW NOVELS

THE PLUNGER. By Hawley Smart. 2 vols.

JACK'S SECRET. By Mrs Lovett Cameron. 3 vols.

A HOMBURG BEAUTY. By Mrs Edward Kennard. 3 vols

CRISS CROSS LOVERS. By the Honble. Mrs H. W. Chetwynd. 3 vols.

BASIL AND ANNETTE. By B. L. Farjeon. 3 vols.

BRAVE HEART AND TRUE. By Florence Marryat. 3 vols.

A WOMAN'S HEART. By Mrs Alexander. 3 vols.

APRIL'S LADY. By Mrs Hungerford, Author of 'Molly Bawn.' 3 vols.

F. V. WHITE & CO.,
31 Southampton Street, Strand, W.C.

THE WAY SHE WON HIM.

CHAPTER I.

DOLLY HEARS A LECTURE.

WHEN Hugh Vavasour, after taking a tender farewell of little Dolly, saw all the members of his family embark afresh upon their return to England, he had made a courageous effort to detach his thoughts from the sweet, as well as the bitter, memories of the past. By mutual consent there had been no farewell

A

meeting between himself and his wife; he had, however, informed the latter in writing, of his intention to see her face no more, and in the letter, by which she realised the fact that the secret she had so long guarded had become known to her husband, he gave forcibly expressed directions that, if possible, his youngest daughter should be carefully kept from the knowledge both of her relationship to Ettie and of her mother's early frailty.

" For God's sake," he in bitterness of spirit wrote, " let the child, in so far as such a thing is possible, respect you, and, for the sake of your own conscience and peace of mind, see that she becomes in the future, a better woman than you have proved yourself to be."

The art of money-making was one which Vavasour had, in earlier days, both understood and successfully culti-vated; now, therefore, that the pas-sion which had of late engrossed him seemed doomed to die a natural death, the self - exiled man turned, with an almost feverish eagerness, to the excitement which had formerly rendered existence enjoyable to him. At the commencement of his new life, the pursuit of wealth was, by him, solely undertaken for the hoped-for result of driving away dull care, but, as his "pile" increased, and the scenes through which he had, during the recent months, been an actor, gradually grew before his mental sight, less highly coloured, the fever of accumulating riches waxed fiercer within his brain, until it was only the correspondence that he punctually kept up with Dot which seemed capable of diverting his thoughts from what had become, *pro tem.*, the main object of his existence.

As a matter of course, he, long before the four years of his bachelor life grew to a conclusion, had become possessed of an amount of wealth which, even in the Argentine Republic, where millionaires are far from rare, was spoken of with bated breath by the gold worshippers and sycophants who, from out the gay and wicked capital of the Republic, spread far and wide the reports of his vast monetary successes.

The fact that her husband had become rich "beyond the dreams of avarice" was not long in reaching the ears of Mrs Vavasour, and her anger was intense in that he showed no signs of increasing an income which, though fully sufficient for her requirements, did not provide for the extravagant expenditure in which it would have been her delight to revel.

" I cannot conceive," she said one day to her daughter, Lady Sundridge, who, from a quiet, modest girl had developed into a harmless specimen of a mildly frisky matron, " what your father can be saving up his money for. I hear from all quarters how immensely rich he is, and yet he leaves me and Dolly to rub along as best we can in our wretched little house in Dynevor Terrace, without a regular carriage, and with a parlour-maid to wait upon us. Whom *do* you think he can be saving up his money for ? "

"Perhaps," rejoined Lady Sundridge simply, "he is not saving it at all. My father may possibly have demands, of which we know nothing, upon his expenditure. You see, mamma, that with two separate establishments—"

"Upon my word, Ella," broke in the indignant wife, "I am surprised at you! Your father's character as a moral man has always been unimpeachable, and now you, his daughter, who, when you married, were old enough to form some judgment of his conduct and principles, are the first to cast a stone at him."

"But, mamma, you mistake my meaning altogether," rejoined Lady Sundridge sweetly. "I had not the slightest intention of blaming my father" (which assertion was, indeed, to a certain extent true, for in "smart" society's lenient code of morality the keeping-up of the kind of establishment the idea of which had roused the wife's displeasure was scarcely viewed in the light of a *péché mortel*), " but we have all, I fancy, formed some idea of the requirements of Buenos Ayres society, and that, in proportion as you make money, you are required to spend it, and I have little doubt that big dinners and entertainments, and an array of servants which that sort of open housekeeping renders necessary, runs away with three-fourths, at least, of my father's probably greatly-exaggerated wealth."

This conversation took place on the day following the recognition by Mrs Vavasour, at the opera, of the daughter whose very existence was in her eyes as a blight and a reproach, and the

scene was the spacious drawing-room
in Grosvenor Place, a mansion in
that locality having, during several
generations past and gone, been an ap-
panage of the Earls of Sundridge. Mrs
Vavasour, after her lengthened illness,
was still weak and in need of watchful care on the part of those about
her, for her malady had partaken of
a nervous character, and an attack
of hysterics — or, as some were unfeeling enough to call it, *temper* —
was too apt to follow on any lengthened opposition, either to her opinion
or her will. Of this truth no one
was more thoroughly cognisant than
Lady Sundridge, but the fact being
that for motives personal to herself,
that astute young matron was extremely desirous that her mother
should suffer no relapse into in-

validism, she lost no time in putting a harmless colouring upon the hint which she had incautiously thrown out. Ella's motive for wishing to keep Mrs Vavasour in a satisfactory state of health was to be found in her own very decided objection to acting any longer the part of chaperon to her younger sister. Dolly was both prettier and more popular than herself; more-over, she danced like a sylph, and her laugh, which disclosed the whitest and evenest of small teeth, was almost as charmingly joy-inspiring as that of Lady Alston herself.

Taking these circumstances into con-sideration, it is scarcely surprising that Lady Sundridge, who was not without pretensions of her own to beauty and to grace, should have been desirous of making over the charge of Dolly, during the gayest, giddiest portion of the London season, to the young girl's legitimate protectrix.

" It will be everything for Dolly to go out with you, for you see, mamma, that I do not quite like to give up dancing," Ella craftily remarked, " and sometimes it has happened that, when *her* dance has been over, I have not been at hand to take care of her You need not remain long, if you feel tired, at Lady Bellinghurst's ball to-morrow night.   It is not to be a crowded affair, and your not being strong will be quite sufficient excuse for leaving the festive scene betimes."

Whilst this colloquy was, on one bright summer afternoon, being carried on, another of a different character · was engaging the interest of two far fairer women, and causing, as will presently

be seen, a flutter of unwonted excitement to stir in the, till then, calm
breasts of both.

Charlie Alston and his wife had, for
their *habitat*, a charming small house
in Curzon Street, and into the pretty
drawing-room of that house, Dolly Vavasour, between whom and Ettie there
existed a warm affection, presented her
pretty self, on the afternoon preceding
the ball, to which (this time under
her mother's wing) the young girl
was to be taken. Ettie had, alike
through respect for Mr Vavasour's
wishes, and from feeling the ex-
pediency, both for Dolly and her
mother's sake, of keeping the latter's
secret, never permitted the vaguest hint
of her own near relationship to Dot to
transpire; nevertheless, in her longing for
the ties of near kindred of which she

envied in those around her, the possession, she had been glad to cultivate her
sister's affection, and even the mere fact
of calling the happy, light-hearted girl by
her baptismal appellation seemed to draw
the child nearer to her own tender heart.

"Well, darling," said Ettie, after the
kiss of greeting had been given and
returned, "so you are come, I hope,
to give an account of your last night's
proceedings. Mind, I expect a true and
unreserved one," she added, playfully
holding up in menace a taper finger,
"for I am afraid, my Dolly, that when
your chaperon was engaged on her own
behoof, you took advantage of her absence
to — what shall I   call it ? — be missing without leave, eh ?   And now, you
naughty child, will you make amends by
telling me with whom it was that you
skedaddled ? "

"It was hardly skedaddling," Dolly, with rather a conscious laugh, rejoined, "for I didn't go far. I was under the big cedar tree on the lawn the most of the time, and any one who chose might have seen me there."

"And Lord Henry—how about that beguiling partner of yours; was he—"

"With me all the time?" Dolly rather defiantly breaks in. "Yes, if I must tell the truth, and somehow I never can fib, Lady Alston, to you. Lord Henry had been my last partner, and, as the room had been fearfully hot, we went together upon the lawn for air."

"Thereby running the risk of a severe cold. If I were your chaperon, child, you should incur no such dangers, and when my Fay is your age—"

"She will be as good as gold, the

darling!" and then, with a half sigh, she added, "I only wish that it could be you, instead of my mother, whom I am now to be taken out with, and," vehemently, "I hate the very thought of it, she is so prying—so hard."

"Hush, dear Dolly," put in Lady Alston gently, "you must not forget that Mrs Vavasour has gone through a long and suffering illness, and that, when the nerves have been shaken and shattered, the character and disposition sometimes suffer for a time in consequence."

"I do not believe that any shaking would change your character," said Dolly fondly to her friend, "so you must at any rate let me tell you that I consider mamma a very bad substitute for Ella."

"Ah, child!" smiled Ettie, "that is,

I fear, because Lady Sundridge allowed you a dangerously long tether, and that now your wings—poor wild bird —will be clipped, and that you will subside into a well-behaved, decorous young lady."

"That I shall never be!" exclaimed the girl excitedly. "I hate hypocrisy, and loathe decorum. Sooner than become the thing you say, I would marry that prig Horace Vane, whose only merit that I can see is that he is a friend of yours."

"I think you wrong him," rejoined Ettie mildly; "and moreover, dear, you must forgive me for saying that a marriage with such a man as Horace Vane does not deserve to be spoken of as a *pis-aller.* In the world's opinion, he stands very high, as well he may, for his mental gifts are unquestionably

of the highest order, and he has already
given proofs, short as his experience
of Parliamentary life has been, of a
brilliant as well as useful career. But
enough for the present of one who
both Charlie and I are proud to call
our friend. It is Lord Henry Tremayne,
dear, that I would gladly, if you will
be patient with me, warn you against.
He is, I admit, handsome and fascinating,
far more so, I can easily understand,
than can appear to a young creature such
as you, our poor Horace; but, child,
I ask you what—in the event of your
giving such a man as he, your heart
—is to be the result to you of a
gift so precious? He cannot marry—
nay, hear me out, and do not go
on torturing those poor little fingers
by reducing that very thorny rose
spray to fragments — for even did

inclination lead him in that direction, which I suspect is not the case, he has, so says report, long ago made away with his younger brother's fortune, and is now so *criblé de dettes* that the bankruptcy court, that last refuge of the impecunious peer, looms darkly before him."

"But," cried Dolly, whose patience—a species of property of which she never had a large stock—was by this time exhausted, "there is really, dear Lady Alston, no occasion to inform me of all this. Marriage and Lord Henry have never been coupled in my mind together. He amuses me, and he dances beautifully."

"And, in the meanwhile, his vanity is gratified by having his name coupled with that of pretty little Dolly Vavasour, whilst she—ah, child! when

I reflect on what your father would think and say could the *chaff* and gossip of the clubs reach his ears, I feel that I must leave no stone unturned to save you from the danger that you are incurring."

The tears were in Ettie's eyes, and her voice faltered as these words of warning fell from her lips. Memories of the blythsome past, when, in the days of her almost childhood, the friend of whom she had just spoken had been her guardian and protector, came thronging across her busy brain, whilst mingled with them were thoughts, bitter and shame-inspiring, of her own mother's early fall, and her fears lest not a few of the older generation might have retained within their memories some echo of the long ago scandal, when, in the columns of the

Satirist, the "fast and flirting daughter of a Furzeshire baronet" was hinted at as having loved unwisely and too well.

Dolly's eyes were also moist—for she dearly loved her father — when she interrupted her friend's appeal by saying penitently,—

"You are very good to take so much trouble, and think so much about me. I would not for all the world do anything to vex my father, and there," with an arch smile, "though I can't promise not to think Lord Henry a thousand times nicer than—er—any one else, I will try to remember all you say, and, after seeing my behaviour at Lady Bellinghurst's ball, no one shall have a word to say against me."

"Bear in mind, please," smiled Lady Alston, as the young girl pressed a parting kiss upon her lecturer's cheek, "that my watchful eye will be upon you;" and a few minutes later, when the mistress of that bright, flower-scented room found herself alone, she mused sadly enough upon the little chance she saw that a girl such as Dolly would be able to resist the temptations by which she was assailed.

"I trust that she will keep straight," Ettie said to herself; "but, alas! she is our mother's child, and in her nature the seeds of evil may have been already sown."

CHAPTER II.

THE income possessed by the Alstons was, taking into consideration the requirements of their position, far from a large one. The principal cause, however, for its inadequacy was to be found in the expensive habits and immense capacity for getting rid of money which, in Charlie Alston, had, from his early boyhood, been one of his distinguishing traits. It was in vain that Ettie, with her shrewd common sense, and honest hatred of debt, en-

deavoured to steer clear of the rocks
and shoals which, when once the fatal
step of "living beyond the income"
has been taken, are apt to beset, at
every turn, the household which that
step—barring some expected and favourable turn of fortune's wheel—has en-
tailed upon it. Like the wise young
woman that she was, she never spoke to
her husband concerning the money worries
which too often caused the pillow upon
her fair young head reposed to be a
sleepless one, while never a hint that
he was in a great measure responsible
for those worries, escaped her lips.

It was to Jennie alone—the Jennie
whom she always regarded and treated
as a sister—that anxious wife sometimes
confided her pecuniary difficulties, and ap-
plied to for advice as to how she could
make tenpence go as far as a shilling.

In the conferences between the pair which took place in the now fashionable dressmaker's private rooms, Charlie's name as a fruitful cause of his wife's anxiety was never mentioned, nor was there indeed much assistance from the housekeeping experiences of Mrs Jem Curtis to be gained, the establishments and modes of life of the two women being necessarily on so widely different a footing; but in the Emporium off the Fulham Road, at the door of which smart carriages laden with expensively got up ladies were now so often seen standing, Ettie was certain to find, both from Jennie and from the still bedridden invalid, a ready sympathy with the difficulty of which, in days of yore, they had felt the pinch, the difficulty, *id est*, of making both ends meet.

During the four years that had passed

over his head, the always remarkable
beauty of which Charlie Alston could
boast, had rather increased than diminished; his manner, too, and conversation,
which had never been deficient either
in grace or charm, had acquired, since
he had mixed familiarly in the best and
liveliest of foreign *coteries*, even a greater
amount of fascination than they had in
earlier days possessed. Those good and
gracious gifts considered, it may well
be credited that their possessor was
looked upon with eyes of signal favour,
both by society in general, and by
the fair sex in particular; nor was the
ex-Household Brigade officer — devoted
husband although he was—insensible to
the pettings and flatteries with which
fair women of *both worlds* were wont
to betray the effect which Charlie
Alston's handsome face and winning

ways had produced upon their hearts or fancies. He came, in fact, of a wild race, for, strictly moral man and somewhat over-exacting father as Colonel Alston after his marriage became, that gallant officer's youth had been a stormy one, whilst *his* father, Sir Henry Alston—a hale old gentleman of eighty—to whose baronetage the Colonel would in the common course of things succeed—had been, in his day, as noted a *viveur* as ever, in the early days of the century, made his name as a successful *coureur des dames* one of evil report throughout the land.

Had Ettie not been one of the few women whose gift of discretion was above the average, it is more than probable that this fiery strain in the Alston blood would have worked mischief in the *ménage* of Charlie Alston and his wife, but the latter, ever bearing in mind the French diplomatist's advice that, *pour bien jouir de la vie, il faœt glisser sur bien des choses,** kept her eyes open to all that was going on around her, but betrayed no signs, either of anxiety or displeasure.

It chanced that, at a period when Ettie's pecuniary worries were being especially trying, and when Charlie, ignorant (so much, at least, must be urged in his excuse) of the burden of cares that pressed heavily on the slender shoulders of his wife, pursued, with a light heart, his career of selfish indulgence and extravagant expenditure, a more than usually attractive *diva* was drawing nightly crowds to the " Liberty" Theatre in C— Street. Miss

* In order to enjoy life, it is necessary to pass lightly over many things.

Zoe Carrington—for such was the *alias* she had chosen—was not a very young woman, but her eyes were magnificent, her figure grace personified, and her dancing simply perfect. But, in addition to these causes for popularity — and the addenda was one of no trifling importance, the favourite *danseuse* of the "Liberty" possessed a ready wit, or rather a pleasant gift of lively chatter, which, combined with no small amount of coquettish daring, rendered her, on the whole, a young woman whom the inexperienced of the other sex would act wisely in giving a wide berth.

Rather unfortunately for Charlie Alston, Miss Carrington, who had an eye for masculine beauty, and a fancy—not an uncommon one with ladies of her class—for thrusting her fingers into happily constituted matrimonial pies, was stricken with an enthusiastic admiration for the handsome husband of the beautiful and once popular Music Hall singer. Lady Alston's early history was no secret, especially to the class to many of whom, not only her well-merited reputation for perfect purity of life, but her extraordinary rise in the social scale, had been objects of bitterest envy; and the idea of making mischief between Sir Charles and his wife found especial favour in Zoe Carrington's perverted sight.

To effect this object was, however, a more difficult matter than was dreamt of by the plotter, for not only was Ettie fully as dear to her husband now as she had been when first he led her from the altar, but there was his love for his only child, the sweet little Fay, whose

childish kisses were more precious to
him than rubies, to stand between him
and harm.

Of this serious hindrance to success
Miss Carrington probably knew nothing,
for, without much misgiving as to the
future, she commenced her campaign
in this wise. She had, on two succeeding forenoons, kept her eye upon her
intended victim whilst he amused himself in the Hyde Park ride, in breaking in as a cover hack, a hundred-
guinea three - year - old, which, regardless of expense, he had lately made
his own.

Zoe was a fearless as well as a
graceful rider, and her bay mare
" Coquette," the gift of one of her
numerous admirers, was as near perfection
as it is possible for a lady's palfrey
to be. In a dark brown habit, which

fitted her classic bust and shoulders, as the saying is, "like wax," she paced leisurely up and down the ride ; but, on the third turn, she, having recourse to an old ruse, and one which Charlie found no difficulty in appreciating, dropped, when within a yard or two of that observant gentleman, the coral - handled whip which she carried. Now, under ordinary circumstances, for an equestrian to dismount and restore fallen property of this description to its owner is the simplest thing in life. In the present instance, however, there existed the complication which the skittish behaviour of a half-broken thoroughbred introduced into the affair. To hold that young animal well in hand the while he picked up the lady's whip, and when presenting it, to duly touch his hat, were per-

formances which, achieved as they were
with the accompaniment of bright "chaff"
and laughter, tended not a little to
facilitate the commencement of an
acquaintance between the parties.

" A thousand thanks," said Zoe,
when, on Charlie placing the dainty
toy in her hand, she flashed a
glance from her splendid eyes into
the face which possessed for most
women a perilous charm; and then
the pair, sauntering leisurely, took
a few turns in the ride together.

It was a harmless "first step"
enough, and yet, neither of it nor
of several succeeding meetings with
the *danseuse* of the "Liberty" did
Charlie Alston make mention to his
wife. For this reticence on his
part, it would have been hard to
find a reason. It may be that he

was feeling just a little flattered
(there is, as you may possibly remember, a dangerous strain in the
blue blood of the Alston race) by
the evident liking and admiration of
Zoe Carrington for himself; or, what
was more probable, he held in such
high honour the delicate purity of
the wife he loved so well, that he
would fain prevent even the name
of the somewhat notorious Zoe
Carrington from reaching, when coupled
ever so innoculously with his own,
the sensitive ears of the woman
who to him had become "still
dearer than the bride."

So Ettie remained in ignorance of
her lord's erratic proceedings, whilst
the *diva* of the "Liberty," with a
tact and prudence for which few
would have given her credit, was

pursuing her destined prey with a perseverance worthy of a better cause. I have already remarked of Charlie Alston that, quite independently of the admiration which his striking beauty of person inspired, he possessed the gift —a perilous one both for himself and others—of almost unconsciously awakening in the breasts of not a few women a warmer feeling than that of appreciation of his good looks. In his dark blue eyes there was the expression, "half languor and half fire," which, in one of Byron's passion-stirring heroines, the great poet has described so well. And then his voice and manner, chivalrous and decided, as well as — when he so pleased — softly caressing, had worked wild havoc in his day in the hearts of the susceptible, one of whom,

to her cost, Miss Zoe, only too
soon, found herself to be ! It
was long, if ever, since she had
felt the thrillings of the tender passion, and that she did so now
was, I think, chiefly owing to a
somewhat singular cause. In all her
past experience, and it had not, in
men and manners, been inconsiderable,
it had never been her lot to become acquainted with so thorough and
complete a gentleman as Charlie
Alston, and it told perhaps somewhat in her own favour that she
was able to estimate at its true
value, a character such as his, and
also to regulate her discourse to
suit his tastes.

It is a proof that the *danseuse*
possessed some tact and clearness of
perception that, bent as she was on

making a conquest of Lady Alston's husband, she never either "forced the running," or led the subject of conversation towards his domestic relations. The very existence of his wife was by Charlie a silently tabooed topic, and it was only through an *apparent* accident that he was led to speak of his other household deity, *id est* his four-year-old darling — Fay. Riding one afternoon in the Regent's Park, Miss Carrington— whose real name, she being a widow, was, as she had previously informed her attendant Squire, "Mrs Bruce"— the pair came suddenly upon the open door of one of the many so-called villas which in London's least popular park are to be found. At the sound of the horses' feet, a little child — a rosy girl, rising four,

ran out, and on the riders coming
to a halt, was lifted, on a sign
from Zoe, by a trim nursery - maid
in attendance, upon that lady's lap.

"My only pet, Sir Charles," said
she, entirely ignoring, as she stroked
the flaxen head of the little one, a big,
hulking boy of some ten years old, who
was relegated, under the care of her
aged mother, to a safely distant country
home; "my little Rosie will be four
next month. Isn't she a darling?"

"She is indeed," responded Charlie,
not untruthfully, for Rosie, though not
to be compared to his golden-haired pet,
could boast of the prettiness which few
healthy children of her age and plump-
ness are ever wholly without. His
thoughts flew homewards, as the child
was held up to him to be kissed, and
Fay, with her bright blue eyes and lovely

rosebud mouth, took, in his imagination, the place of that more robust - looking, and coarser-built little one. And not in his imagination only, but, as the pair rode homewards, in his manner of speech. For when it became a question of describing Fay, the father's tongue was loosened, and he said enough in praise of that peerless little maiden to convince the woman who, with well-acted sympathy, listened to his words, that the most formidable rival in a contest for Charlie Alston's heart was to be found in the little child who was so innocently unconscious of the havoc in men's hearts which, later in life, it would probably be her lot to work.

CHAPTER III.

DOLLY MAKES A DISCOVERY.

" CHARLIE, dear, if you have no objection, I am going to write to-day to Mr Vavasour."

So speaks one evening, towards the close of the London season, Ettie Alston to her husband. They are both in their respective rooms, making ready for a dinner at the Austrian Embassy, to which function they had been for several weeks past, the invited guests. The door which separates their respective apartments is not closed, therefore even Ettie's voice, "soft, gentle and low" though it is, reaches her husband's ears, and, for the reason that he has always entertained a vague although unspoken suspicion of Vavasour's real feelings towards his wife, he answers her remark somewhat curtly, as he arranges his white neck-tie before the mirror.

"What are you going to do that for? You have never written to him before, have you?"

"Never. Nor should I do so now" (and, as she speaks, she, in her pretty blue cashmere dressing-gown, makes good her entrance into her husband's sanctum, and seats herself upon a low arm-chair), "were it not for Dolly's sake."

"For Dolly's sake? Why, is there anything the matter with the child?"

"Yes, dear Charlie, and very much the matter too, in my opinion, for I fear that she is falling desperately in love with Lord Henry Tremayne."

"You don't say so? That would be a misfortune. But what reason, darling, have you for fearing that it is so?"

"Her whole conduct, poor child; I grieve to say. I cautioned her once— it was the night before Lady Bellinghurst's ball, and advised her, for as strong reasons as I could venture to bring forward, not to do anything which could possibly give rise to talk. Well, she promised to be careful, and on that one evening she behaved well enough, only danced with him twice, and was not once, as she had been only too often before, found with him in conservatories and balconies. And I can see a change in her. She looks worn and anxious, and oh, Charlie dear, when I think of the past—"

"Yes, it's a bad look out, I fear, my pet," broke in Charlie, who never could bear to see a cloud on his wife's smooth brow, or a tear in her bonny blue eyes; "but what good can writing to Mr Vavasour do?"

"Why, it will bring him home when I tell him of Dolly's danger. He has the greatest influence over her, whilst her mother—how I shrink from calling her mine!—has less than none."

"But," resumed Charlie, who, with all his kindly interest in his sister-in-law's future, could not view the possible return, at his wife's summons, of Hugh Vavasour without the recurrence of painful thoughts, "would not a letter from him to Dolly answer the purpose? Surely he could write and forbid her to see Lord Henry again. If, as you say, his influence over Dolly is so great—"

"It would do no good," Ettie, with a sorrowful shake of her small head, responds. "Letters—especially from such a distance as Buenos Ayres—would avail nothing. Mr Vavasour must come home, and he must act as he will see fit for poor Dolly's good."

"Poor Dolly, indeed," repeated Charlie to himself, whilst putting the finishing stroke to his toilette. "Troublesome, naughty little puss; she deserves to have her ears boxed for falling in love with a reprobate like Tremayne, whilst such a rattling good fellow as Horace Vane is dying—more fool he—to have his innings."

On that night, nothing more passed between Charlie and his wife about the missive with which, the latter hoped, in all wifely loyalty, and without a shadow of a guess at what had passed through

her husband's mind, would bring Dot's
anxious parent to the rescue. Ettie
had played her conversational part so
well at the big ambassadorial dinner
to which the *élite* of London society
had been bidden, that none present
could have guessed, whilst listening to
her lively sallies, and the pretty laugh-
music which rippled from her lips, that
deep in her heart more than one secret
sorrow lay; and Charlie, too, although
his part was a comparatively easy one,
deserved some credit for the manner
in which he contrived to hide from all
present the fact that not a few of his
past follies had begun to find him
out.

In a certain carefully locked *escritoire*
which lurked behind the door of his
smoking den in Curzon Street, there
reposed, in fact (the major part of them

being still hermetically wafered) such an array of blue tinted-*reminders* as Charlie lacked the courage to calmly contemplate. Those ominous-looking *envelopes* did not, as I think I need not say, contain household bills, or were they connected in any way with Lady Alston's personal expenditure, but were simply the result of Charlie's inveterate habits of extravagance, among which habits, a taste for bestowing expensive presents to his friends, cut no mean figure.

As the couple, who had by their beauty of person and charm of manner contributed more than their quota to the success of the banquet, drove home in their brougham, Charlie Alston, gay as was his habitual temperament, could almost have echoed the sigh that broke, despite her efforts to conceal her depression, from the lips, which of late had become slightly lined with care, of his fair young wife.

Before she sought her couch that night, Ettie had written to Vavasour the letter from which she hoped so much. In that letter, after reverting in a grateful spirit to all Hugh's former kindness towards herself, she represented to him,. in no mild or measured terms, the danger which his little Dot was running. She described the character —an utterly unscrupulous one—of the man who was obtaining, as she feared, a fatal influence over Dolly, and expressed in strong terms her own opinion that the girl's father, and he alone, could, in the present crisis of her life, save her from destruction. "She loves you so dearly, poor child," Ettie, with tears falling unwiped upon the paper, wrote, "and would not willingly grieve or pain you, so that if you will, on receipt of this letter, hasten home, all may yet be well; and I pray you, if you can, to pardon my anxiety, and the strong terms which I have felt compelled to use. Dolly is very dear to me, and I tremble, when I remember whose daughter I am, to think of what may be my little sister's fate."

This letter, the substance of which is here given, was duly, on the following morning, posted for Buenos Ayres, and, after its despatch, Ettie carefully counted the weeks which must perforce intervene before Hugh Vavasour could obey her summons. Ill luck, however, apparently attended the step she had taken, for, some little time previous to the date when Lady Alston's letter reached its

destination, Hugh Vavasour had started
on a long and wandering tour through
Central and Northern America to San
Francisco, and thence possibly to Japan.
Under these circumstances, it is not
surprising that Ettie should have waited
in vain even for the answer by telegram
which she had requested might be sent.
In the meantime, she kept as best she
could, watch and ward over her young
sister, a labour of love, however, which
was soon brought to a close by two
events, the first of which I shall now
in due course relate.

On the third morning after the despatch of Ettie's letter to Buenos Ayres,
as she was sitting before her davenport, and wearying her brain as usual
with calculations which brought a pucker
across her low white forehead, and a
tired look—early as was the day—to

her lovely eyes, the door of her morning - room was suddenly opened, and
Dolly entered with a rush, and flung
herself on her knees beside her friend.
For a moment or two she seemed unable to speak, but soon she drew her
breath more freely, and then the words
that she had come to say, poured forth
as in a torrent.

"Oh, *ma mie!*" she cried, addressing Lady Alston by the pet name which
the latter had chosen for her to employ,
"I have heard such dreadful things,
and I have come to you to ask if
they are true. If they are, I shall
hope and pray to die, for I could not
live and bear them."

"Hush, my child," said Ettie gently,
as she passed her hand caressingly over
the young girl's ruffled locks, "and try
to be calm, so that I may be able to

understand what has happened, and what it is that you, who I have always looked upon as such a courageous little woman, have so promptly decided that you cannot, or rather, I suspect, *will* not exert yourself to bear."

Thus adjured, Dolly began a tale which Lady Alston, in much distress of mind, listened to in painful silence.

" It was at Mrs Crichton Bonner's reception last night that I heard, while I was in a sort of tent on the balcony, my name mentioned. When one does that, there is no harm, is there, dear, in listening ? "

" I do not know. I cannot tell you now. Go on, dear," continued Ettie, with an amount of impatience rarely displayed by her, "and let me know what you heard."

"It was late, and there were only a few people left. Ella, who had brought me to the party, was in a downstairs room talking to Mrs Crichton Bonner, and probably the two men, one of whom I knew by his voice to be your friend Mr Horace Vane, thought that I was either with Ella downstairs, or gone away home. If they had not believed me to be safe out of hearing, the one who was *not* Mr Vane would not have said (as the two leant together over the balcony railing), 'It is a pity to see a girl so young as Miss Vavasour—such a mere child, in fact—making herself conspicuous as she, from pure thoughtlessness, is doing. Were she the child of any other mother it would, of course, matter less that she should be intimate with such a *roué* as Tremayne.'

" 'Ah!' said Mr Vane, and I could

hear that he spoke in bitter anger, 'as long as the poison of asps lies under human lips, so long will poor weak women be the sufferers from its venom. Surely, after eighteen, nay, even nineteen, years, it is time that the wretched story to which you allude, might be buried in oblivion.'

"'As it would probably have been, my dear Racy,' said the other man, 'if it had not been for the girl's own folly. She is a flirt—a harmless one, I admit, but a very charming one— and girls such as she are terribly apt to provoke the enmity of their own sex; and it is so easy for the mothers of unmarriageable daughters to hint at bygones and heredity, etc., and so that miserable scandal—'

"'It would be more to the purpose,' broke in Mr Vane passionately, and oh!

dear, his words seemed to cut my heart like a knife, 'if some one who has a right to take that poor child's part would rather more than hint to the selfish villain who has dared to compromise her that he is the dishonourable scoundrel that every honest man must feel he is. If only her father—' but at that moment a voice from below calling loudly for 'Horace Vane,' put a stop to the conversation, and," the girl added, fixing her large, resolute eyes on her companion's face, "now I am here to ask you whether what those two men said is true."

It was a trying question; nevertheless, Ettie found herself equal to the occasion. She had long been aware that, sooner or later, Dolly must learn the truth, and now that the discovery was coupled with a certain amount

of salutary enlightenment as regarded
the man whom she had set up—poor,
foolish maiden—as an idol to be worshipped, the prudent young matron felt
rather relieved than otherwise to find
the ice broken, and her own task—
painful although it was—rendered thereby comparatively easy. During a few
rapidly fleeting moments, she employed
herself in passing in review the circumstances attendant on the terrible revelation to which Dolly had been an
ear-witness, and she arrived at the
conclusion that much must "stand
over," until a more convenient season
for its being made public, should
arise. Still, even taking into account
these advisable reservations, there was
so much to say that could not fail
to wring with shame and anguish
the hearts of both women, that Ettie,

when she prepared to answer the queries which had been put to her, was conscious of an hysterical rising in her throat which she could not, without an effort, either swallow or drive away.

CHAPTER IV.

" My poor child," said Ettie, when she had told her melancholy tale, "I am grieved for your sake that you should have had this sudden shock—"

"Oh, please not to mind that," interrupted Dolly, who, seated on the rug at her friend's feet, was looking up eagerly to that friend's pallid, sympathetic face; "only tell me whether the woman of whom these two men spoke is the one whom I have hitherto called my mother."

"And whom, my darling, if I know

you well, you always will call by
that most sacred name ; for, child,
because the world has been cruel, and
that, nineteen years ago, she was deceived and compromised by one of
those selfish profligates who, for the
gratification of their own tastes, care
not one whit what misery they may
bring upon the woman they profess to
love, it is not for us to be her judge."

"And my father," faltered the girl,
"did he know, when he married, of
this shameful story ? And was there—
no, I cannot ask it! Only tell me
one thing more, and I have done.
Was it all made public ? Were there
no attempts made to screen her—er—
misfortune from the world at large ?"

"Indeed there were, and most successful ones. It was only by the
Alstons and one other person con-

nected with them that the affair was
known. I cannot tell you that there
were no surmises, for we know how
ready every hand is to throw a stone,
but—"

" But you—*you* knew it; and this
morning, when I thought that horrid
conversation over, it came into my
head that, the first time you spoke
to me about being careful, you were
thinking of—my mother. Was it so?"

" Yes, dear, and having married an
Alston, who—but we have talked enough,
and more than enough, on this sad
subject, Dot," continued Ettie, who, not
being a practiced dissembler, felt herself floundering into deeper waters
than she cared to trust herself in.
" You must try, if only for your
dear father's sake, to forget that you
ever heard that colloquy. A child should

not sit in judgment on a parent, and you should strive to feel pity rather than blame for one who has had, you may be sure, her share of suffering."

"Oh, if I thought that," said Dolly, and the remark was thoroughly character-istic of the girl's nature, "I should feel differently, but mamma has not suffered, or if she has, it has only made her hard and pitiless. I am certain—now you must not be shocked, *ma mie*—that if I were to be in—"

"Hush! for heaven's sake, Dolly; for a child like you even to think such things is terrible enough, but to give utterance to them—"

"Is only what is to be expected from my mother's daughter," the girl ejaculated bitterly, and then for several minutes there was silence between the sisters, one of whom was far as the poles are asunder from surmising the close relationship that existed between them.

At the expiration of those minutes, Dolly spoke again.

"I promised," she said, "to ask you no more questions, but there is still one which I must entreat that you will answer. If you refuse, I must go for information to my mother herself. Who is the man, that I may hate him whilst I live, who brought this dishonour upon one who must, at that time, have been a girl little older than myself?"

Ettie's reply came slowly and very sadly from her pale lips.

"I cannot tell you, dear, for I have promised secrecy, and promises with me are sacred things; but as regards the per-

son of whom you have spoken, I have
this to say, you had better reserve
your hate for one who, in my opinion,
deserves it more, and who being—
contrary to his deserts—still living, may
possibly cause you to, one day, experience its effects.   The man about whom
you have just questioned me has been
long since called to account at a higher
tribunal than ours for sins which, there
is reason to believe, he repented of
before he died."

What was it, think you, that, deprived
of their sting the only words even
bordering on bitterness that ever left
the tongue of the tenderest of her
sex?   Reader! you have but to remember that she spoke of the man
to whom she owed her birth, and my
question has received its answer.

Dolly, thoughtless child although she

was, had not listened without a sensation of awe to Lady Alston's im-
pressive words; she was struck, too,
by the pained and harassed expression
which had crept over her friend's
face, and therefore decided that to
leave that friend to the healing effects
of solitude would be, for her sake, the
better part. Acting on this resolve,
she rose from her crouching position,
and said, very tenderly,—

"How I *have* been tormenting you,
you poor, pale thing! But I will
go now, and you must not think
any more about my troubles," and
having so said, Dolly, pressing a loving kiss upon her mentor's cheek, left
her, as Ettie hoped, to the melancholy indulgence in her own thoughts.
Such hopes, however, were destined to
prove unfounded, for the door was

reopened softly, and little Dot's blonde head made its appearance at the aperture.

· "What is it, dear?" asked Ettie, advancing to the *rencontre*, for she felt far from equal, just then, to another agitating interview, with Dolly's perplexing questions taxing to the utmost her powers of dissimulation.

"Only this, and forgive me, for I am so miserable, for troubling you again. Does Ella know," she whispered, "and Sundridge? Oh, I hope not; he is very good, but cold and hard, and he has looked at me lately as if he thought me such a dreadful sinner! It would kill me quite, I think, to hear *him* say of me—'Like mother, like child.'"

"Which you never will hear, dear, from his lips, for Sundridge is too

true a Christian to be uncharitable.
No, dear Dolly, I think I can say
positively that Ella and her husband
know nothing of this sad story. However, as I may, after all, be mistaken, I advise you to be careful—
more careful," she added, with a
smile, "and a better - behaved little
lassie altogether than you have lately
shown yourself to be."

"Indeed I will," Dolly, with tearful eyes, rejoined ; and then, with
another affectionate embrace, they parted,
this time, happily for Ettie's sake,
not — for the present, at least — to
meet again.

.   .   .   .

At that period of her life, Lady
Alston was more often alone than
was altogether good for her. London,
although Goodwood races were not

yet over, had more than begun to empty, and Charlie's frequent absences from home, at Sandown or Kempton Park, and such like gatherings, filled his wife's mind, especially in her lonely hours, with a vague uneasiness. Dearly as she loved him, and the more, perhaps, because of her great love, did she understand and make allowances for a certain weakness of character which was the result, in a great measure, of natural kindness of heart, and of a dislike to giving the degree of annoyance to others which so often tends to diminish the popularity of the donor. Yes, Ettie had become well aware of the fact, not only that her husband liked popularity, but that he enjoyed, rather more than was altogether safe, the excitement of a bet. That any of

the hours of his now frequent absences
were spent in the companionship of
a handsome, unprincipled free - lance,
his wife did not for a single moment
suspect. When at home, it was so
abundantly clear that his love for
her and for his child had not been
diminished by a shade, that Ettie
was justified in believing — as, with a
sorrowful heart, she in silence did —
that the gloom which occasionally
darkened Charlie's handsome face was
due either to unsuccessful turf ventures,
or to a cause, the hateful pressure of
which she was only too well able
to realise — the pressure, that is to
say, of unpaid and unpayable bills.

Ettie had never given her careless, pleasure - loving husband credit
for any extraordinary readiness to
satisfy the just demands of the trades-

men whom he employed, and there
had been occasions when he, having
brought home expensive presents either
for her or Fay, she longed to ask
him whether or no the pretty bracelet or the charming little sealskin
paletot, trimmed with blue fox fur,
had been duly paid for. To put
such queries, however, she found, when
the moment of trial came, utterly
beyond her power, for she too had
her weak points, and amongst them,
the dread of giving a moment's annoyance to Charlie was one of the
most salient.

She is thinking of that weakness
now, as, after Dolly's final departure,
she locks up her davenport and prepares for a drive in a hired victoria
with little Fay and her French maid,
Josephine, to the Park. It is a

lovely afternoon, and as all the world,
including, as she imagines, her husband,
will be away at Goodwood, Lady
Alston, as she takes possession of
her iron chair, with little Fay prattling by her side, and Josephine—from a
respectful distance—looking on, rejoices
in the thought that for an hour or
two, at least, she will be enabled,
without the tiresome interruption of
unsympathetic acquaintances, to think,
with the hopefulness which is part
of her nature, of the future that
lies before her.

CHAPTER V.

A RUDE AWAKENING.

IF the reader of these pages has been led to imagine that in Charlie Alston's breast there existed even the faintest glow of tenderness for the graceful dancer, whose fame as a performer was rapidly extending to the Continent, a very false impression of my hero's character must unwittingly have been given. He was, as I said before, flattered, and even touched by a preference which the lady did not attempt to conceal, and which was, in fact, too dangerously real to be

easily feigned; but although this was
the case, the strongest feeling with
which association with Miss Zoe Carrington (*alias* Mrs Bruce) inspired
him, was one of bitter regret that
he had not, on the occasion of their
first meeting, spoken openly to Ettie
of that trifling event. That he had
not done so was in part owing to
the exaggerated sense of loyalty to
the sex which, whether the individual
in question were worthy or otherwise
of chivalrous treatment, had always
marked his conduct. And if, when
this daring specimen of the *demi-
monde* had as yet only shown for
him a coquettish, and perhaps merely
passing fancy, a sense of honour
prevented the betrayal of her advances,
how much the more did he shrink,
when the nature of her feelings

towards him became evident, from revealing to any soul that lived the extent of the weakness he deplored.

"How can I thank you enough," the love-lorn *diva* is murmuring to him one afternoon.

It is the great day at Goodwood, and they are riding together in the deserted Row, Charlie being employed, as many a better and worse man has been before him, in the endeavour to make amends, by tenderness of look and manner, for the loving words with which he is incapable of responding to the fair Zoe's utterances.

"It was so good of you," she added, "to give up the races on my account. But indeed I should not have dared ask you to stay away, had I not been going abroad so soon. I wish now that I had not accepted the Paris offer. It's so awfully hard to be forgotten the moment one's back's turned, and I shall know no one in France to make amends for what I leave behind," and a long, wistful glance from her splendid eyes said more even than did the low-voiced words which had fallen from her tongue, of the regrets with which her ill-regulated heart was full. Now, to utter encouraging and responsive whispers to a woman whose love has failed to strike a sympathetic chord is, as I have already hinted, at no time an especially easy matter, and it was in a rather hesitating and bungling fashion that Charlie Alston said,—

"I am sorry that you do not look forward with pleasure to your trip, but it will be different when you once find yourself in the swim. Paris is an awfully jolly place, and as to being forgotten, I am not likely to forget old friends, or the pleasant rides that we have had together."

The consciousness that his words were lacking in warmth was probably the reason why Charlie, whose hand was now on the pommel of his companion's saddle, endeavoured to make amends for the absence in his response of earnestness and fervour, by leaning, in what might well pass for a lover-like attitude, towards the not unwilling ear of the *danseuse.* Whilst thus occupied, and his attention being wholly absorbed by the difficulties of his position, he failed to notice a quiet figure seated near the Park railings, and this although *her* eyes were fixed upon his movements, and that a child, his little Fay, whose back was towards the riders, was leaning on her mother's lap, engrossed in the pages of a new picture book.

But, although Charlie's attention had been too much engrossed for him to perceive the presence near him of the gentle lady from whose beautiful face every tinge of colour had for the moment fled, the eyes of the woman to whose ear he had been whispering were keener far; and, by Zoe Carrington, the graceful figure of Charlie Alston's wife was recognised at a glance. More than a week had elapsed since the Music Hall *danseuse* had, without much difficulty, discovered the abode of one who, with a feeling born of bitterest envy, she had brought herself to hate. She had watched Lady Alston, too, as she stepped into her carriage, and had recognised in her the *grande air*, and refinement of bearing which, in Charlie Alston's manner, had the salutary effect of keeping her own gushing emotions in check. The sight of little Fay, moreover, had contributed its quota to swell the volume of poison which filled the plebeian veins of Zoe Carrington. That small fairy, with her wealth of golden hair, threw, as Rosie's mamma could not but reluctantly own to herself, that young lady's charms into the background. The appearance of rude health which was characteristic of Zoe's child was perhaps wanting in Fay, but, on the other hand, Lady Alston's little daughter looked thoroughbred from the crown of her golden head to

the tips of her tiny shoes, and the
soi-disante widow therefore hated her
with a hatred such as only a woman,
thwarted and jaundiced by envious pangs,
is capable of feeling.

Charlie Alston, in blissful ignorance
that his wife had been an eye-witness
of his whispered converse with a woman
who, to her at least, was a stranger,
escorted his late companion to her
home ; whilst she, on her part, was
mindful not to disturb the equanimity
he seemed to be enjoying by any
allusion to the fact that she, more observant than himself, was cognisant of
the discovery which Lady Alston, at
the eleventh hour, had made. That
the latter would, in the natural course
of things, reproach her husband for his
duplicity and ill-doing, the sharer in
that duplicity felt well convinced, and

with that conviction there came to her
the heart-breaking truth that the days
of her companionship with the man
who, all unwittingly, had filled her breast
with a passion as dangerous as it would
probably be fleeting, were at an end for
ever.

In this, however, she was mistaken,
for during the next day, and the one
following, Sir Charles chose the Regent's
Park as the arena of his morning ride,
whilst, during the last of those two
much - prized visits, he brought with
him, in default of a more sentimental
gift, a *trifling souvenir*, as he called
it, of the rides which Miss Carrington
had rendered "so agreeable." He was
a *grand seigneur* in his way, and was
accustomed to pay for any pleasure
which the fair sex afforded him; consequently, when he presented the brace-

let, the cost of which was ten guineas, to the lady who in a week's time was to dance at the Gymnase Theatre for the pay of thirty pounds per night, his conscience did not reproach him for any act of disloyalty towards his wife.

.   .   .   .

Meanwhile, how did Ettie comport herself under the shock — for shock it had been—which she had received? In truth, not over bravely, albeit she strove her utmost to carry a bold front before an unpitying world. She bore the burden of this fresh sorrow, even as she had done those of others, in silence ; the said burden being rendered lighter by her firm belief that nothing more blamable than " weakness " could be laid to her husband's charge. Some shameless woman must, she felt, have fallen in love, even as she had done, at first sight with her Charlie's handsome face. "Poor boy," she said to herself, "I cannot wonder; he has such winning ways, and may not have been proof against her seductive flattery."

Apologies such as these, the poor young wife kept repeating to herself, but although, in very truth, she did not fear that Charlie's affection for herself was one atom lessened, yet she shed not a few bitter tears over the concealment which he had practised towards her; and, strive as she might, she could not altogether conceal, from one who watched her sweet, expressive face so lovingly as did Charlie, that she was not altogether happy in her mind.

A week had elapsed since the memorable scene in Hyde Park, which Ettie had unsuccessfully endeavoured to banish from her memory; and before another eight days would have glided by, Charlie's inamorata would— not a little, it must be owned, to his satisfaction — be crossing the Channel, *en route* to her Parisian triumphs. It is the breakfast hour in Curzon Street, and little Fay is, as usual, disporting herself round the table, and occasionally opening her rosebud of a mouth to receive such proportionate dainties as her " daddie " thinks fit to offer for her acceptance. Now, as a rule, on the like occasions Ettie showed herself very carefully on the watch to prevent any excess of liberality on Charlie's part towards the pretty little creature who, like a young fledgling, stood with open eyes and mouth beside the parent bird, waiting to be fed. So accustomed was the latter to Ettie's

mildly sounding but authoritative re-
monstrances, that, when he found himself permitted, without interference
from his wife, to indulge Miss Fay's
extravagant demands, he looked with
surprise at the quiet face behind the
tea urn.

"Why, darling," he said anxiously,
for it needed no prolonged gaze to
convince him that she looked pale
and sad, "what has happened? You
surely do not mean to let Fay and
me follow our own devices without
a check? No, pet" (this to the
little one), "you have had your
share of good things, and we must
see after the mumsey now. Why,
my child," leaving his half-finished
breakfast in order to draw a chair
close to that of his wife, "you have
eaten nothing, and you don't look

like yourself. Has anything happened
to worry you? Fay! you little greedy
puss, leave the marmalade spoon alone.
By Jove" (this *sotto voce*), "what
a torment the dearest of children
are sometimes."

"Perhaps, dear," suggests Ettie, in
her quiet way, "you had better ring
the bell for Josephine. It is nearly
time for Fay's walk, and I confess
to having something of a headache."

"Nothing worse, are you quite
sure?" Charlie inquires anxiously.
"Not been disquieting yourself about
Dolly, or—er—anything else?"

It would have been well for Ettie
could she, at that moment, have
summoned courage to reveal to him
the hidden causes which were begin-
ning to draw lines of care along
her brow, and to banish the faint

carnation hue from her delicate cheeks;
but, as we have seen, she too is,
in her way, a moral coward, and
as she cannot, without implying ill-
doing to Charlie, talk to him either
of accumulated bills, or the episode
in the Row, she tacitly pleads guilty
to having had her rest disturbed by
Dolly's unfortunate discovery.

"I began wondering," she says,
"whether Ella Sundridge *has* any
knowledge of the truth, and then
it occurred to me as strange that
Dot did not question me more
closely about many things than she
actually did. It was indeed a blessing
that she did not, for I should have
been sorely puzzled what to say." •

"I suppose," rejoins Charlie, "that
the man who was talking to Horace
Vane must have been his brother

Fred; but, upon my soul, darling, there ought to be a law—a kind of statute of limitation, don't you know—against raking up those old-world scandals; and if I were Vavasour, not even my love for my child should drag me back, after the awful discovery he made, to England. He would probably be forced to see his wife again—"

" Ah, I can well understand his dreading *that*," Ettie, with a kind of suppressed shudder, ejaculates; "for one of the worst evils of my position is the necessity of casual meetings with *her*, which I cannot always avoid. To feel—or rather to know—that she is my mother, and to pass her by as a stranger, is — but I must not dwell, dear Charlie, on this ' crown of sorrow.' With so many compensating blessings for which to be thankful — with your love first and foremost—" (and the culprit, thus addressed, did not, despite the giving of that pretty, unpaid - for trinket either blush or grow pale as he met his wife's fond gaze)—" and darling Fay—"

"You must not forget *my* people," interrupted Charlie; "for both my parents love you as dearly as though you were their own child."

"They are very, very good to me," Ettie says feelingly, as she watches her husband's practised fingers whilst they manufacture the cigarettes with which he is about to fill their accustomed case. "Shall you be back for luncheon, dear?" she asks, a little wistfully, as Charlie, his daily task ended, presses a tender kiss upon lips which care has not rendered less ripe and lovely than of yore.

" I don't know. Perhaps not. If it keeps fine, I am due on Tad-caster's coach, to Hurlingham. But do you be sure to go out, darling, and let me find more colour in those dear cheeks when I come home at seven."

Ettie hears the door close upon his departing footsteps with a sigh, and, feeling her loneliness oppressive, she rings for Fay; but the little one has been taken for her morning walk, so Lady Alston retreats to her own sanctum, where, but for the recurrence to her memory of the following sensible lines, she would probably have enjoyed the so - called luxury of tears :—

"Oh, how idle to talk of indulging in grief! Talk of indulging in
the rack — the rheumatism! Who
that has ever felt it can wish to
indulge in grief? To endure is hard
enough."

CHAPTER VI.

CHARLIE MAKES A CLEAN BREAST OF IT.

THE hours passed slowly and sadly for Ettie, whose thoughts were now with her husband amongst the gay companions and temptations of Hurlingham, and anon, against her own wish and will, with the strange woman into whose bold face she had seen Charlie gazing with eyes which the "creature" herself might easily have mistaken for love. For almost the first time in her life, she found herself incapable of employment. If she attempted to read, her thoughts strayed from the page before her, whilst the little frock, a garment of many colours which she was embroidering for Fay, fell from her listless fingers as though it had become a thing of no account.

In the midst of her far from satisfactory reveries, she was startled by the sound of the luncheon gong, and then, and not till then—so absorbed had she been in her own thoughts—did she begin to wonder why Fay had not, as usual, made her appearance after her walk, for the spelling lesson in which both mother and child took delight. "Josephine is keeping the child out too long," she was saying to herself, and then, not for the first time, the idea of diminishing the household expenses by giving "warning" to Josephine, of whose conduct she had lately found reason to disapprove, crossed Lady Alston's mind. An instantaneous thought, truly, for at that moment the woman herself burst, without previous notice, into the room, exclaiming as she did so, in her own language, and with frantic gesticulations,—

"Oh, my God! my God! The little one is lost. It was not of my fault. We crossed the street, and she had my robe in her hand. She would never let me lead her, and some one must have caught her up whilst I was look-ing to see if it was safe to go to the other side."

All this information, and even more, did the garrulous Frenchwoman pour forth, before Ettie, who seemed paralysed by the shock, arrived at any clear understanding of the terrible calamity which had befallen her. It was the housekeeper, a woman of middle age, who also acted in the capacity of cook, and who, on hearing that "something was the matter," had followed on Josephine's steps, by whom the unhappy mother was restored to sense and feeling. Mrs Guthrie was an old retainer of the Alston family, and, seeing the condition of her young mistress, she felt herself justified in taking vigorous measures for her recovery.

"A glass of wine, quick!" she said to the butler, who also felt privileged by his position to see what was going on, "and take that chattering French-woman from the room."

These orders having been promptly complied with, Mrs Guthrie having also succeeded in inducing her well-nigh cataleptic mistress to swallow a few mouthfuls of old Madeira, assisted in placing her slender form upon a couch; and these remedial measures, aided by perfect quiet, had shortly the effect of restoring Ettie to something approaching to a sense of what was passing round her.

"What has happened? What did Josephine say?" the poor mother, with a dazed look in her lovely eyes, and pushing her hair from her forehead, asked.

"You'd best keep quiet a bit, milady," said the housekeeper. "You've had a fainting fit, and Dr Fancourt has been sent for, and when he comes he will say what is best to be done."

"But what," asked Ettie, whose senses were only too rapidly returning, "did Josephine say about the child? Was it— oh, my God! I remember now!—that she has lost my darling? Send for her at once, and, whilst I am able to bear it," she, with a wild hysteric laugh, added, "let me know the truth."

Whilst Josephine, the state of whose nerves was likewise the reverse of satisfactory, was being sought for, Mrs Guthrie, with the best intentions, was endeavouring, by banal reasonings such as never yet blunted the edge of grief, to calm the growing excitement of the agitated mother.

"Don't you, now, milady," she said, "take on this way. Miss Fay may be brought home, for what we know, in half an hour's time, and if she isn't, why, a big reward will bring the little dear back in no time, we may be sure of that."

It was a fortunate circumstance for

Ettie that Josephine's entrance on the scene and that of Dr Fancourt were simultaneous. The latter was not only a shrewd, practical man, but an old family friend, so that his very presence had a reassuring effect on Ettie. He endorsed Mrs Guthrie's opinion as to the effect of a reward, and sent off, at Lady Alston's request, a telegram to Hurlingham, requesting the immediate presence of Sir Charles in Curzon Street. It was in vain that efforts were made to elicit from the French-woman any more particulars of the deplorable event than those which she had already given. The crossing at which the child had been missed was, it had been ascertained, that at the Stanhope Street gate, and Joseph-ine, whose nerve, when brought in-to the presence of her mistress, utterly

failed her, had, it appeared, enlarged
in her broken English to the servants
below stairs on the wilfulness of Miss
Fay, when a street, however crowded,
was to be crossed, on taking care
of herself. "*La petite est si contra-
riante,*" she declared, "*que c'est
vraiment étonnant qu'un malheur pareil
ne soit pas déjà arrivé.*" *

Now, little Fay being a remark-
ably gentle and obedient child, the
mention of this new trait in her
character occasioned some little · surprise amongst the household. The
accusation, however, remained unknown
to the higher powers until circumstances connected with the loss of
little Fay called, later on, attention
to the Frenchwoman's invidious re-

* The child was so disobedient that it was really
surprising that a similar misfortune had not already
happened.

marks. Infinitely to Ettie's relief, and, indeed, somewhat to her surprise—for the subterfuge on the Goodwood Cup day had remained stamped upon her memory — the telegram despatched by Dr Fancourt was successful in finding, amongst the fashionable crowds at Hurlingham, the individual sought for. The dispatch sent, gave, as may be mentioned, no particulars of what had actually occurred, but the mere fact of his being sent for, even had not the signature of Dr Fancourt been appended to the missive, was sufficient to set the father's brain on fire with anxiety and terror. In truth, the mental tortures which on his progress homewards he endured, were, methinks, almost sufficient punishment for the follies which, by Miss Carrington's wiles, he had been induced to commit. It is an old saying, and one which, in words at least, I have never heard disputed, that "anything is better than suspense." Let me, however, ask any unfortunate one who has gone through the tortures of uncertainty, whether—could he be given his choice —he would not willingly exchange them for the dreadful truth which had taken their place, and his answer, in ninety - nine cases out of a hundred, would, I trow, be in the affirmative.

Charlie's impatience to reach his home was such that his state of mind, as the driver of the hansom cab pulled up his panting horse at No. 90 Curzon Street, bordered on frenzy. Throughout his short and rapid journey he had seemed to himself to crawl, so eager was he to learn the reason of his summons, but when the truth was told him, and when he learned that in that big, cruel London city, with its many millions of inhabitants, his little darling — his dainty Fay, on whose cheek no wind had hitherto been allowed to play too roughly — was actually *lost*, his grief and fury knew no bounds. So great, indeed, and so alarming was his excitement, that it acted beneficially on his wife, who was reminded by her alarm on his account that, although bereaved and sorely tried, there yet remained to her one whose existence was precious as rubies in her sight. So, for love of him, and in the hope of raising him from the depths of despair into which he was plunged, she mastered her own mental agony, and spoke words of comfort to the excited man.

She found him in the smoking-room, closeted with Dr Fancourt, and endeavouring, with shaking fingers, to write a copy of the handbill in which a description of little Fay was to be published abroad, together with a reward of fifty pounds for her restoration.

" Let *me* write it, darling," Ettie, who had entered softly, and laid her hand upon her husband's shoulder, whispered. " I can describe the dress better than you can," and she took the pen from his unresisting hand.

Charlie stood behind her as she wrote, trembling visibly.

" Write 'bright blue eyes and golden hair,' " he faltered, and then, for the first time, there came to him the relief of tears, and, throwing himself into an armchair, he wept the scorching drops which only fierce mental torture can wring from a strong man's eyes. No such relief had as yet been accorded to the poor young mother, who, with orbs dry and burning, stood beside the stricken man, murmuring in his ear words of encouragement, whilst her own heart was breaking with the grief which was not, for the sake of that other, allowed to have its way.

"She will come back soon; money will bring her, will it not, Dr Fancourt?" she kept repeating as though mechanically, whilst the "Surely, surely" of her interlocutor came with monotonous regularity from the lips of the worthy man, who had already exhausted, in his attempts at consolation and encouragement, every topic which had presented itself to his mind.

"Who shall venture to describe the

mental sufferings which followed for the unhappy parents on that never-to-be-forgotten day? At the commencement of their terrible ordeal, they were sustained by the hope that the large reward (it had been increased by swift degrees to five hundred pounds) which had been offered for the restoration of little Fay, would bring her back to her parents' longing arms; but as the days and weeks succeeded each other, and no tidings of their darling came, hope died gradually in the hearts of the waiting ones, and the sufferings of long - endured suspense began to tell visibly upon both—upon Ettie the most severely, seeing that her health was delicate, and that she had, poor young creature, to find courage for two. One source of consolation alone remained to them, namely, the certainty, as the police and those in authority over them declared, that no street accident could be the cause of their little one's disappearance.

"Why, Sir Charles," the stalwart men in blue had repeated *ad nauseum* to poor Charlie, "if a child dressed as was your young lady had been runned over by a 'ansom, or one of them murderous butcher's carts, it would have been in the evening papers, and all over the town the next day. Whoever's got the little Miss is treating of her well, you may be sure, and the reward offered is certain to bring her back afore long."

These repeated asseverations produced some effect in calming the anxiety of the father, but the vivid imagination with which Ettie was, for her misfortune, endowed, effectually prevented her receiving comfort from the arguments which, emanating as they did from Scotland Yard, he, with the idea of inspiring his broken - spirited wife with something approaching to hope, invariably repeated to her. The haunting thought was hers that Fay, the loving mother's child, whose tender ears had never since her birth listened to a harsh and fear - inspiring word, might, alas! now be in the power of some virago who, not content with threatening, might — ah! God in Heaven forbid!—torture the delicate flesh, and bruise the wounded limbs of her heart's darling. Fancies and terrors such as these were frequently effectual in banishing slumber from her eyelids, and on one night, when the sounding voice of "big Ben," had proclaimed the fact that two hours past midnight had sped by, she was startled by the discovery that Charlie's place by her side was empty.

A bright harvest moon was lighting

up the room, and, by its clear, cold rays,
she swiftly donned a dressing gown
and slippers, and, striking a match,
hurried downstairs to her husband's
smoking-room. He was seated at a
table, on which stood a reading lamp,
while a mass of papers were strewed
about. Her entrance was unobserved,
for in her velvet slippers she stepped
very softly, and Charlie's head, as he
leant over the table, was buried in
his clasped hands. For a minute she
stood in silence, watching his lowered
brow, but a convulsive sob, the out-
come of deep-seated remorse and grief,
found an echo in her own breast, and,
leaning her fair head upon the shoulder
of the grief-stricken man, her small white
fingers caressed, as gently as though they
were little Fay's, his short chestnut curls.

"What is it, my own?" she softly

breathed. "Surely nothing that your own Ettie may not hear?"

He raised his head, and by the dim light, saw her, more beautiful in that simple, clinging robe than ever in Court costume, with diamonds on her neck and brow, she had seemed to him, and yet he dared not clasp that slender waist, or meet her questioning gaze, for on that very day there had come to him, with other pressing reminders of his selfish extravagance, the jeweller's bill for Miss Carrington's bracelet, and, on taking courage to look into his affairs, he ascertained the fact that, owing to his reckless carelessness, the change of air and scene recommended by Dr Fancourt for Ettie could not, in consequence of lack of funds, be undertaken.

Once again she spoke.

"Darling," she whispered, and this time her voice had in it the sound of a caress, "could you speak to me more frankly if you knew that your prying little wife is already, she thinks, mistress of your foolish secret? Nay, you need not start, dear, it is not much of a secret after all. I saw you once riding with a— er—a stranger, and I was sorry, that was all. And now, will you be very good, and tell me as much of the story as you would like me to know?"

Thus encouraged, Charlie took heart of grace, and with his sweet wife's hand in his, confessed the sins—not very heinous ones, after all of—which he had been guilty. His conscience, when all had been said, was lightened of a load, and thenceforward, with the exception of the one great and undying sorrow, which they bore

as best they could, together, there occurred
nothing to disturb the domestic peace of
Sir Charles Alston and his wife.

Together they formed plans for
future retrenchment. Charlie's two
hundred guineas' cob was sold at
Tattersall's, and happily for little less
than the sum which it had origin-
ally cost, and one man-servant, instead of three, assisted one another
in the arduous task of doing nothing. Both the pretty brougham
and the light victoria were, to Ettie's
relief, sent to the auction rooms,
and thenceforward, when it was necessary that she should drive out, a
hired brougham was at her service.
Their establishment was shorn of its
splendour, but they were no longer
in debt, and Lady Alston's conscience
was thenceforth at rest.

CHAPTER VII.

TRUE OR FALSE.

" PLEASE, Sir Charles, there's a person below who gave in this card, and says he would be glad to speak to you," said Becker, the Curzon Street serving-man, with a countenance big with solemn meaning, as he presented a card on a silver salver to his master.

" Tell him I will be down directly, Becker," rejoined Charlie, who had, as Ettie had not failed to perceive, become a shade paler as he scanned the card.

" He has brought news of Fay ! I am sure of it," she cried ; " and oh, Charlie, let him come up here. I will be very good, and will not utter a word whilst you are questioning him."

There was something in the expression of the servant's face, stolid although it was, that caused his master to hesitate, a proceeding on his part which rendered Ettie more desirous than ever to have her way.

"Let me come down with you, then," she said; "but tell me first, dear—this man comes from Scotland Yard, and has news to give us—is it not so?"

She spoke so calmly that Charlie deemed it advisable not to disguise the truth.

"Yes, darling. But it would be better perhaps for me to see him first alone—"

"No, no! I could not bear it," she exclaimed excitedly, her powers of self-control being for the moment exhausted. "Whilst you were hearing what the man has to say, the suspense would drive me mad."

Then Charlie yielded his will to hers, and the policeman in plain clothes, for such the new-comer was, followed the stately Becker to the drawing-room upstairs.

He was a keen-faced man of some forty years of age, and his glance at Ettie as he entered the room, did not escape Charlie's notice, and increased his regret that he had been unable to give the man a private audience. However, it was now too late for change, so he began the colloquy as follows :—

"You have, I suppose, some information to give regarding our—loss ?"

"Yes, Sir Charles," said the man hesitatingly. "A discovery has been made, and as it is a question of identity—"

"Oh !" broke in Ettie, forgetful of

her promise to be patient, "why was she not brought here at once, that we might decide the question for ourselves? Where is the child? Can we not go to her immediately?"

The man's discomfiture at this question was so evident that Charlie, who also could scarcely control his growing agitation, felt convinced that the discovery which had been made was not one likely to give hope and comfort to those who were mourning over their darling's loss, and therefore, for the first time since his marriage, he spoke with an air and voice of authority to his wife.

"My dear, this discovery may or may not be one of importance, but, whatever it may be, I think it advisable that I should first ascertain what there is to learn. You may be sure that I shall not keep you long in suspense, so wait here patiently till my return." And, having so said, he signed to the policeman to follow him from the room.

.   .   .   .

As Charlie Alston preceded the stalwart policeman down the stairs, along which little Fay had so often merrily tripped, the sense of coming disaster was so strongly impressed upon his mind, that his face, bronzed by exposure, had grown white to the lips, and large beads of perspiration were standing unwiped upon his brow. Nevertheless, his pride enabled him to say calmly,—

"I could see, policeman, that what you have to tell had better not be told, without preparation, before Lady Alston; but *I* am ready to hear what the discovery is of which you spoke."

"Well, Sir Charles," replied the policeman, whose distaste for the office he had to perform was made clear by his evident attempt to pull himself together, "there may be something in it, and there may not, but when the lady talked of seeing the child—why, sir, barring the little thing's hair, there's not a feature in its face that is, as one might say, as nature made it."

"I do not understand your meaning," faltered Charlie, who had grown, during this suggestive description, scarcely master of his emotion. "Is the child you speak of dead?" and a strong shudder, which he strove in vain to suppress, ran through his frame.

"Yes, Sir Charles, and has been so these six weeks or more, the doctor says. The body was found yesterday by some boys who were fishing for gudgeon in the Thames, near Isleworth. It had been caught in the weeds, and, as the doctor said it was about the age of your little one, it was thought best—though, as I said before, there ain't much, barring the hair, to know it by—to let you know as it was found."

The well-known frequency with which the waters of the Thames are known to give up, after a certain period, their dead, supported, in some degree, Charlie Alston's courage during the short but terrible details to which he had been listening. The bodies of poor little superfluous children were so often, as all the world knew, consigned, chiefly by their brutal parents, to the tender guardianship of the "Father of Waters," that he saw no reason to believe that the small unfortunate of whom the policeman spoke was the darling whom he and his wife still sought for sorrowing. One circumstance, however, staggered him, namely, the time—six weeks, according to the doctor's computation—that tallied cruelly with the period which, since the loss of little Fay, had elapsed. It was this circumstance, together with what had been said about the dead child's hair, which decided him to accompany the policeman to the mortuary, and there, terrible as would be the ordeal, judge for himself whether or no the drowned child bore any resemblance to the bright-eyed little one that they had lost. Before taking this step, however, it behoved him to see Ettie, and, if possible, allay the state of excitement into which, by the advent of the policeman, she had been thrown.

"It is nothing, darling," he, assuming a careless air, said, "but one of the

old false alarms, or rather hope-raisings.
A poor little child has been found in
the river, and although by the description it bears not the slightest resemblance
to our lost darling, yet I think it better
to go with the man."

"You are quite right, dear," Ettie,
with a composure which astonished her
husband, said assentingly ; "and, Charlie,
darling, if you have any reason to think
that the poor little one you are about
to see is our sainted child, do not
try to hide the truth from me. You
will think, perhaps, that the agony of
these last weeks has unhinged my
mind, but indeed it is not so. It
would be such a relief to think of our
little Fay as safe from earthly injury—
safe, my Charlie, in the bosom of her
Father and her God, that, if you can
bring back any token that so it is, I

shall thank the Almighty on my knees for His great mercy."

Her manner, which was, to Charlie's thinking, unnaturally calm, frightened him not a little, and, but for his appointment with the police officer, he would have remained to mount guard by her side. Circumstanced, however, as he was, his only resource was to desire Mrs Guthrie to be on the watch, and as his road to the mortuary lay by Dr Fancourt's door, he delayed the hansom for a minute, in order to beg that trusted *medico* to pay, without delay, a friendly visit in Curzon Street.

Charlie Alston, albeit physically as brave as are most Englishmen, had not, as must have been already seen, been gifted by nature with nerves of steel, and it is hardly too much to say that he would have preferred being ordered on the

famous Balaclava death-ride to looking
upon the sight which was about to meet
his eyes. It had never been his lot to
witness the gruesome spectacles which
of necessity familiarise the eyes of
many with the various forms of death,
and that on which he must now force
himself to look was, he had been
taught to believe, one of the most
terrible in which the grim destroyer
ever invests his pale and ghastly form.
He was no Hotspur, I grant you, this
hero of mine; but when we remember
how dearly he had loved the little
daughter on whose disfigured remains
he might be forced in that dismal
charnel - house to gaze, methinks that,
under similar circumstances, the courage
of few fathers would have better stood
the test.

It is soon over, that greatly dreaded

ordeal, and before twenty minutes had
elapsed, Charlie is again in Curzon
Street, carrying with him very carefully, but still with a certain repellent
sensation which he finds it hard to
overcome, a long straight lock of light-
coloured hair. It has been cut from
the head of the drowned child, and,
making due allowance for the long
continued action upon it of the water,
might once have borne a resemblance
to the waving golden tresses which in
life had crowned the head of little
Fay. Charlie had thought it his duty
to carry this terrible memento to his
wife, in order that she might decide
for herself in what light to view this
only, and, in Charlie's opinion, highly
unsatisfactory, evidence of their child's
decease. To his surprise, however, Ettie
saw in that dull, discoloured tress the

proof for which, in her restless, feverish heart, she had begun to pine. She insisted on being informed of the period during which the child had been, according to the doctor's belief, in the river, and his conjectures likewise as to its age was confirmatory of her fixed idea that little Fay was, as she expressed it, "Not lost, but gone before."

It was in vain that Charlie endeavoured to combat this article of faith, and after a while, seeing that the conviction she entertained was one from which she derived comfort, he ceased from combating it; and thus it fell about that, whilst one parent continued with all the energy of his naturally sanguine nature, to *hope*, the other, who, partly from her own experience, and partly from the anxiety which, on Dolly's account, she was still en-

during, had conceived exaggerated ideas
of the dangers to which youth and
beauty are exposed, found consolation in
the thought that the "flower she most
did love" was safe from earthly hand-
ling; and Charlie, as he watched her
in her sleep, and saw again the smile
upon her perfect lip which had long
been a stranger there, almost rejoiced
in what he deemed her infatuation,
whilst he repeated half aloud, as he
gazed on her now tranquil face, the
Poet's Wish :—

> "Bright be thy dreams, may all thy weeping
> Turn into smiles whilst thou art sleeping,
> May the child whose love lay deepest,
> Dearest of all, come whilst thou sleepest.
> Still the same—no charm forgot,
> Nothing lost that God had given,
> Or if changed, but changed to what
> Thou'lt find her yet in Heaven."

CHAPTER VIII.

DURING the long season of trial and suspense which followed on the loss of their child, no visitors, with the exception of Dolly and their own relatives, were received by Charlie Alston and his wife. Their most frequent caller, and the one from whose visits they derived the greatest amount of satisfaction, was Horace Vane. His family was closely connected with that of the Alstons, and as for reasons into which it is not necessary to enter, Horace was well aware of the circumstances attendant on Lady Alston's birth, and her consequent near relationship to

Dolly, there subsisted between him and the members of Colonel Alston's family a freedom of intercourse from which outsiders were naturally debarred.

Between Horace Vane and little Fay also there had always existed the warmest friendship.

"We had been pals ever since she could walk alone," the big barrister would say, "and I am not going to give in to the notion that I am never to see her sunny face again."

Impressed with this belief, Horace, with infinite trouble, and assisted by a clever and well-paid detective, traced to its birth and death the history of the drowned child.

"It is not one," he said to Charlie, "that I should like Ettie to hear; besides, till she gets her own child back again, she is happier nursing that poor unfortunate's lock of hair than she would be if her faith in that dismal fable could be shaken. It is wonderful what freaks imagination will play. Why, Charlie, it would be long enough, I think, before either you or I could mistake that discoloured flaxen lock for one of Fay's bright golden curls."

"You forget, my dear fellow," rejoined Charlie, who, feeling that the reputation (a well deserved one) of his wife for common sense was being attacked, took up forthwith the cudgels in her defence, "that in Ettie's case the wish was father to the thought; she was for ever picturing to herself little Fay in the hands of some dreadful baby farmer, who, for purposes of her own, starved and beat our darling cruelly. It was in vain that I argued the point with her. A woman of that description, I

used to say, would be the last to
remain proof against a big reward, and
we may be certain that, whoever has
possession of the child, makes as great
a pet and idol of it as—"

"As you did, old man, eh? Well, I
can believe that. Only a heart of stone
could be hard enough to ill-use little Fay."

The month of September has nearly
waned, and the heat and oppression
of London at its dreariest would long
ere this have driven far away from it
both the men whose colloquy I have
been narrating, were it not that within
the precincts of the overgrown city there
existed, not only for Sir Charles, but
for Horace Vane, an object of interest
which was rarely, if ever, absent from
the minds of each. They are in Hyde
Park now, and sauntering along the
broad walk which skirts the still lovely

flower beds. Not as yet have chilling winds and fogs perceptibly dimmed the brilliant colours, scarlet, pink and yellow, of the well-guarded blossoms, and the two men, but that their hearts and minds are engaged with other subjects, might have found in the gorgeous display which was so soon to be exchanged for barrenness, a topic on which not without sadness, to dilate.

After a silence of many minutes, Vane is the first to speak again.

" It is strange, is it not," he asks, " that nothing has been heard of Mr Vavasour? Is he usually so dilatory a correspondent? And to what does Ettie attribute his silence?"

Charlie shrugs his shoulders, an action not common on his part; but then, for reasons that are unsuspected by his companion, the memory of Hugh Vavasour is one that finds little favour in his sight.

"I do not know," he answers; "she seldom speaks of him; peradventure he is on a journey, or maybe he sleepeth."

Vane looks at the speaker with surprise.

"Why, old man," he exclaimed, "you do not speak of him as though he were the friend I took him to be. Is there anything wrong with the man? I have been looking forward to his coming home, as Dolly's protector and adviser, with such keen anticipations of future benefit that I should indeed be disappointed if, besides being an object of the deepest pity, Mr Vavasour should be unworthy of compassion."

"Which I am far from saying he is," responds Alston; "indeed, I ought to be

the last man living to throw stones at
Vavasour. The poor fellow is, as you
say, awfully to be pitied, but the discovery of the trick that had been
played him was a comparatively late
affair, whereas— Well, well, there are
things which had better be forgotten.
Let the dead be buried out of our
sight, and the past be amongst the
things which have passed away. Above
all things, do not let me prejudice you
against Vavasour; he is a good and
kind father, and I feel persuaded that,
directly he receives Ettie's summons, he
will hurry home to the rescue. I was
not only jesting when I spoke of his
being on a journey, for he is really
extremely fond of travelling, and may
just now be in Japan, for anything we
know to the contrary."

" In Japan ! Good God ! why, it may

be months before Ettie's letter reaches him, and, in the meantime, that scoundrel Tremayne is having it all his own way."

"You know, do you, that he is in London ?"

"Yes, and if I could have brought myself to play the spy on her, I would, as I could easily have done, have made certain that the villain is still at his ungodly work. Charlie, you will, I fear, think me an abject fool, but the thought of her danger absolutely unmans me. I would give a year of life for the right to protect her—"

"But, my dear Vane," interrupted Alston, "have you no confidence in the girl herself? Pardon me for saying so, but I think that want of trust would soon cure me of love for any young lady, however deep, which I had been so unfortunate as to experience."

"Do you think so? Well, if we are to believe the love stories, true and false, of the past, they tell a different tale. That, however, does not affect my position in the least, and I believe that I only speak the truth when I declare my conviction that, were I certain never to see Miss Vavasour's sweet face again, I should still see with dread the danger she is incurring, and hope and pray that she may yet be saved."

"I think, as well as believe, that you overrate the danger," rejoined Charlie. "The child's fancy is touched, and she imagines, I suppose, that she is in love. Ettie has, I know, a better opinion of Dolly than to believe her capable of disgracing herself, and if I did not share in that opinion, I might already — though,

I

of course, I have not the slightest right to interfere — have given Tremayne a piece of my mind. In the absence of her father, Sundridge is certainly the person to whom she has a right to look for protection ; but then, you see, not only is he one of the unco' guid, but he is, I imagine, singularly in the dark regarding the part played by his own father in this lugubrious family history. After all, my dear boy," he added, after a pause, " you are either a singularly bold man, or you have no faith in heredity, otherwise you would hardly be so awfully keen to take one of the Fareholme - cum - Sundridge race to wife."

Again there was an interval of silence. A hiatus which, like another bygone one, was rendered less embarrassing by reason of the cigarettes which sent forth upon the balmy air their quota of wholesome fragrance, and lent a shadow of excuse for the delay in replying to a question that was not without its perplexing side. Horace Vane, however, who was not greatly troubled either by shyness or backwardness at repartee, had his answer ready.

"Your example, my dear Alston," he said, "would, I should imagine, encourage a far more timid man than I am, to set the doctrine of heredity at defiance. I rather fancy myself as a reader of character, and it would require but a very short acquaintance with Lady Alston's disposition to convince me that, unless under very peculiar circumstances, a sister of hers would be as safe from pollution as herself."

" And those peculiar circumstances, eh ? "

" Are the persevering attempts of an arch - devil such as Lord Henry Tremayne to gain an influence over her affections. There are men born into the world for no other purpose, as it seems to me, than to lead women astray. There is something fatal in their very glance, and the brilliancy and daring of their conversation seems to possess a charm for even the purest of girls, which renders all remonstrance powerless to avert the mischief which it seems their mission to work."

" The fellow is atrociously good-looking, too. I wish to Heaven poor Dot had never seen him."

" And to think that this man, less than two years ago, married a pretty innocent heiress of seventeen ! He had no prospect before him but the bankruptcy court, and so sacrificed himself — as he has been heard to say—for an income of seven thousand pounds a year, which enables him to lead the life of pleasure for which alone he has a taste."

"Unfortunately, his being a married man prevents Dolly from seeing the danger she is running. Were he a bachelor, her pride would be up in arms at the idea that she was suspected of angling for a husband. It is difficult to enlighten a child of seventeen, so absolutely ignorant of evil as is Dot, on the real nature of Tremayne's pursuit. Very painful, too, is it to hold up to her, in warning, her mother's early fall."

"Ah, that mother! How little has she shown herself worthy of being trusted with the guardianship of such a child as Dolly—"

"Hush! here comes Ettie herself, and, as I live, with a telegram in her hand. What have you there, pet? Any good news to tell us? We do not deserve to hear it, after leaving you alone so long."

She approached them slowly, after her step had never, since her great sorrow, resumed its elasticity, but there was a smile upon her lip which recalled to her husband the image of the joyous Ettie whom, in her earliest girlhood, he had wooed and won.

"It is from Mr Vavasour, dear," she answered, putting the telegram into Charlie's hand. "He had only just received my letter, and will be here by the first steamer that sails from Rio, homewards."

CHAPTER IX.

THE WANDERER'S RETURN.

"AT last! Ah! how glad I am!" exclaims Ettie, as, with both hands extended, she advances to greet her girlhood's friend.

The steamer in which Hugh Vavasour had taken his passage from South America had not been four-and-twenty hours at Southampton before he put himself into the express train for London. Ettie's accounts of Dolly's flirtation had been too cautiously worded to occasion him any unnecessary amount of alarm. He gathered from them (she having mentioned no names), not that an unprincipled *married* man was striving

his utmost to obtain a dangerous hold on
Dolly's affections, but that a suitor every
way undesirable was offering himself for
her acceptance. Under these circumstances, that the traveller's first visit should
be paid to Lady Alston was the most
natural thing in life, but as the express
train whirled him along towards London,
it is to be feared that, fond as he was
of Dolly, his thoughts were less occupied
by that young person's love affairs than
by the meeting to which, in Curzon Street,
he was hurrying. He had telegraphed
from Southampton a request that Dolly
might be in Curzon Street to meet him,
and now, a man greatly altered in appearance from what, four years before, he
had been, he, with a heart beating as
fiercely in his breast as though nearly half
a century had not shed its snows upon his
head, was about to meet again the girl, now

his rival's wife, who had first, in his middle
age, taught him what it was to love.

"If I had received your letter, I should
have been here before," said Vavasour, as, still
retaining within his own her slender hands,
he gazed hungrily upon her still beautiful face. "It was not till I returned from
San Francisco," he continued, "that I heard
of your great grief, and I longed—I can never
tell you how ardently—to be in England
that I might strive to help you. Poor child!
Poor young mother!" and the voice of the
grey-haired man was very tender and caressing; "God knows I would have given half
my life to bring your darling back to you."

It was not often now that thoughts
of little Fay brought tears to the bereaved mother's eyes, but the mention
of her by her old friend reopened the
sluice gates, and she murmured, between
her quiet sobs,—

"I wish you could have seen her. She was in life as beautiful as the little angel which, I hope and trust, she is in Heaven, now. I have been happier since I knew that she is safe; and that reminds me, dear old friend, that before you see Dolly—"

She is interrupted by the sudden entrance of the young lady in question, who, with an exclamation of, "Darling father, what joy! How long you have been away!" flung herself into his arms.

"Why, what a tall girl you have grown!" he, after taking a survey of his handsome daughter, exclaimed. "You impertinent puss! you must have beaten Ella hollow, if I remember rightly."

"I am two inches taller," Miss Dolly answers proudly. "But oh, father," in a tone of consternation, "what have you

done to make your hair so grey? It
was quite black when we left you."

"Hush, child!" laughed Ettie, "or
your father will think that your growth
in wisdom is out of proportion to that
of your stature. You will dine with us
to-day, I hope?" addressing Vavasour;
"and this child knows that she is always
welcome. I am going to leave her with
you now, for this is Charlie's hour for
his morning ride, and one of my doctor's
favourite prescriptions for me is a canter
before luncheon in the Park. My
husband will have smoked his cigarette by
this time, so, *au revoir*. Take care of your
father, Dot, till I come back, and don't
ask him any more saucy questions, or he
will wish himself back again amongst the
Buenos Ayres beauties."

"Not much danger of that," thought
Vavasour, while he watched the tall, grace-

ful figure, with hair and complexion so purely English, of the young wife, as, with her never-to-be-forgotten smile, she glided from the room. He forgot, as he gazed, the errand on which he had come, and said, in a tone of absorbed interest which did not escape the notice of quick-witted Dolly,—

" Lady Alston talked of a doctor. Has she been ill? She does not look to be so. I am surprised, after all she has gone through, to find her so little changed."

" You would indeed have thought her lovely if you had seen her before the loss of poor little Fay. At the Marlborough House ball, there was no one half so beautiful, and her dress was exquisite ; but she has grown thinner since that time, and Dr Fancourt wants her to go abroad — to Aix, I think —

but she cannot be persuaded to leave London."

"It is not like her to be so determined; but, perhaps—am I right, my dear?" asked Vavasour—"she has remained in London on your account. It is in keeping with her unselfish character to do so. From something that she wrote to me, I fear that my Dolly has not been so prudent as she ought to have been."

"What did Lady Alston write to you, father?" the girl, blushing hotly at the question, asked. "She ought not to have told you anything without first consulting me, for indeed, after she spoke to me about—er—*him*, I was very careful not to do anything that she thought foolish."

"And who, pray," Vavasour, with a half smile, asked, "is *him?*"

"It is nobody," stammered Dolly, "that you know."

"But I suppose," said Vavasour, who, with his arm round his young daughter's waist, was seated on a sofa by the fire, "that I must some day make the gentleman's acquaintance; that is to say, if I am to form an opinion as to whether he is a fitting husband for my child. Come, who is he, Dot? or must I ask your sister—"

"My sister!" cried Dolly, in amazement. "Why, father dear, of whom are you talking? Not of Lady Alston, surely? How can she be my sister? I have always heard that she was quite a poor girl, and became a Music Hall singer to support her family."

"And you heard rightly, as far as the world has been made aware of

her parentage," answered Vavasour, who,
now that he had inadvertently let
fall the family secret, felt it incum-
bent on him to throw a further light
on the mystery of the Past; but when
it came to the point of revealing to Dolly
the story of her mother's fault, both his
courage and his sense of what was due
to the girl herself held him tongue-tied,
and he checked himself abruptly.

"Oh, father, please do tell me how
dear Lady Alston can be my sister.
I have always loved her so much,
but that we have been sisters in
reality I never dreamt," persisted
Dolly, who was too thankful for the
chance this opportunity afforded her
of delaying her father's commenced
inquiries regarding her admirer to be
in any hurry to drop the subject of
her relationship to Lady Alston.

Poor Mr Vavasour, who felt himself on the horns of a dilemma, could imagine no other course to pursue than that of frankly owning his folly in that he had, by a slip of the tongue, betrayed a fact which it had behoved him to keep secret. With this end in view, he said decisively,—

"My dear Dot, you must perceive that Lady Alston's birth is a subject which it is painful for me to discuss with you, and therefore—"

But, by this time, Dolly, who was not more slow of wit than are the majority of young ladies of her age, had, by putting two and two together, very nearly arrived at the truth. If, she reasoned,—Lady Alston were indeed her sister, then the dear "*ma mie,*" who had warned and counselled her, must be the child of one or other

of her parents. That the said parent
was her father, the girl, who on
board the *Princess Carmen* had not
been blind to what was passing
around her, could not bring herself
to believe possible; but, as the discovery which she had accidentally
made of her mother's early wrong-
doing recurred to her, she, little
reason although she had to feel tenderly towards that mother, felt the
blood rise tumultuously to her cheeks,
and, with an involuntary movement,
she stole her hand into her father's,
and held it firmly clasped.

"Don't say any more, dear," she
whispered. "Ettie shall never know
what you have said to me, and if you
will promise not to be very angry with
me, I will tell you who it is that she
warned me not to be seen so much with."

Vavasour, in full expectation that the name he was about to hear would be that of some penniless young soldier, who possessed nothing more valuable than his "kit" to settle on his bride, gave the desired pledge, and then heard, to his uncontrollable dismay, that the dangerous individual who had been laying close siege to his daughter's heart was a married man!

But for his promise, curses both loud and deep would, then and there, have been hurled at the head of the offender; and it was only by a strong effort that Dolly's indignant parent succeeded in adhering to the compact which he had made.

"But, my dear Dolly," he at length, having mastered in some degree his wrath, contrived to say, "surely, when you gave so much encouragement to the man as to give rise to public gossip, you could not have known that he was already married?"

"Indeed I did, father," rejoined Dolly innocently. "Had it not been for that, I should not, I think, have danced with him so often. But oh, father dear, he does waltz so beautifully! Like an angel, I was going to say, but I suppose that angels do not dance; still, I should have been afraid that people might talk if—if— Well, dear, I mean that, being married, it could not be said that I was hoping to be Lady Henry Tremayne; and till Ettie spoke to me—and oh, to think of her being my own sister! But who was it? You will not mind my asking that, dear, will you, as Ettie spoke of him as if he were dead."

He answered her half-finished question in a tone as low and reverential as that which she had herself used.

"Yes, he is dead. He was, as you may have guessed, no other than Lord Sundridge—"

"Ah, I see it all now!" the girl exclaimed excitedly. "I know what Mr Vane and another gentleman meant when I heard them talking about me and mother! Oh, poor father, what you must have suffered! Ettie tried to make me believe there was nothing really wrong; but I can see now the reason why she avoids Ettie, and why she would not let Ella marry Sundridge. I will never, never see her again—you will let me go back with you, won't you, father?" Dolly continued passionately; but her father declined her proposal, gently but very firmly.

"No, child," he said, "what you ask can never be. You owe your first duty to your mother. Whatever injury she did to me I have forgiven long ago, and with that you have nothing to do. I believe that the subject which you unfortunately heard spoken of is known but to very few, and it must not be by means of her own daughters that, so late in the day as this, the gossip—if gossip there has been—should be revived."

"But, father," persisted Dolly coaxingly, as she stroked with her soft palms the bronzed hands of the only parent for whom she felt a daughter's love, "you cannot mean to be so cruel as to go away from us again. I can understand partly, I am afraid, about my mother, but you

have me and Ella, and" (this with
some hesitation) "darling Ettie, who,
if she is our sister, must be the
same almost to you as a daughter.
You could remain near us, you know,
and," with her pretty smile, "see
that your silly Dot does not make
a fool of herself again."

Vavasour had not listened without
much inward perturbation to Dolly's
untimely mention of Ettie's name,
but he betrayed, as he rose slowly from
the couch, no symptom of emotion.

"You will need a good husband to
do that, my child," he, pinching her
rosy cheek, playfully said; "and now,
as I have no end of business people
to call on, and as I shall see you
again at dinner, I must be off. The
Sundridges are living in Cavendish
Square still, I conclude?"

"Yes; but won't you stay a little longer? You used to like your five o'clock tea, and Ettie's cousin Horace Vane is almost certain to be here then. He knows you are expected home, and wants so much to know you."

"Really? Well, I am afraid," Hugh Vavasour said drily, "that he must wait for another opportunity of gratifying his curiosity."

And having so said, he, after bestowing a paternal kiss on the disappointed Dolly's forehead, took his departure, not, as he had informed that credulous young lady, to visit the gloomy haunts of city men, but to wander aimlessly about the Park, wondering whether Ettie—who, in his eyes, was more beautiful than ever— had really been as glad to see him as she had seemed to be.

CHAPTER X.

HORACE VANE GOES A-WOOING.

As I have already said, Horace Vane had always maintained a firm belief that little Fay was not irrevocably lost, and there were moments when he more than half persuaded the sorrowing father that there existed good and sufficient reasons for the faith which he professed. In the first place, Vane, albeit with true legal caution he did not openly give voice to that opinion, had always more than suspected Josephine's complicity in the child's abduction. He had in his own family come across instances of the extreme cupidity of foreign servants, and of Frenchwomen

in especial, who being in receipt, when
in England, of far higher wages than
they can, as a rule, in their own country
earn, labour diligently during a certain
number of years at their vocation, gaining, meanwhile, a wholly undeserved reputation for devotion to their employers,
but never losing sight for a moment
of the main, or rather of the sole, object
of their lives, namely, that of realising
the amount of capital which it had
been their original purpose to lay by.

"I can't quite understand," Vane would
say in confidence to his friend, "that
a less shrewd woman than Josephine
might have been tempted by the high
reward that was offered to pursue different tactics from those which I suspect
her of being capable of, but we must bear
in mind that avaricious Frenchwomen of
her class (and there are no such grasping

devils upon earth) are as cunning as they are greedy. She must be well aware that she has not in the matter of little Fay's disappearance escaped suspicion, and if, as I imagine, she has the child in safe custody, she will wait until the poor little thing's memory has become dimmed by time before she takes any steps about claiming the reward."

"It is possible," mused Charlie, "that she has left England and taken the darling with her. By God! the thought of her being in that terrible woman's power is too awful."

"Take my word for it," rejoined Vane, "that, whomsoever she is now with, that person is not Josephine. That individual, if I have guessed rightly at her purpose, is to act the part of an utter stranger until she feels firmly convinced that the events of that horrible day have faded from the memory of her charge."

"Poor little darling," exclaimed Alston, the tears dimming his eyes as the image of his lost child is thus brought forcibly before him, "how frightened she must have been! And how she must have begged and prayed to be taken back to her home, and to those who loved her."

"Happily," said Vane, "children possess, as a rule, short memories, and the spoiling and petting with which I have no doubt she was, by Josephine's accomplices, treated, will before long have reconciled her to her new surroundings."

"That in itself is a grievous misfortune," said Charlie bitterly.

"But a less deplorable one than that of imagining her to be either dead or a victim to ill-usage," retorted his companion, and then the friends, who had been sitting *tête-à-tête* over their wine in Curzon Street, rejoined Lady Alston, they having confirmed a compact, previously made with one another, that her present state of melancholy resignation was not to be disturbed by any allusion to the hopes which Horace Vane's sanguine expectations had awakened in the breast of his friend.

.   .   .   .

It is Christmas time again, and as more than a year has elapsed since little Fay's joyous voice has welcomed the children's holiday, the hope of once again seeing his golden-haired darling has even in Charlie Alston's breast, died out.

"Whomsoever she is with has grown too fond of her to let her go," he remarked gloomily to his friend, when the latter announced his intention of taking a run over to Paris, and witnessing, as he phrased it, the " humours of *le jour de l'an.*"

"Not a bit of it," rejoined Horace, " Josephine is only biding her time," and he continued—for the two men were together in the young barrister's chambers — to thrust, in the temporary absence of his valet, his travelling kit helter-skelter into a huge portmanteau ; " perhaps— who knows, stranger things have hap- pened—I may bring you tidings of the child."

"God grant it!" ejaculated Alston fervently, "for something tells me, old man, that if good news do not reach us soon, they will come too late. Have you not noticed how changed Ettie has become of late ? She has grown so pale and thin ! For my part, I had never much hope of that belief of hers in the child's death consoling her, excepting for a time, perhaps, for its loss. She has never recovered it, and in my opinion she never will."

"I trust, ay, and I believe, that you are wrong," rejoined Vane. "I do not myself perceive the change you speak of."

"Ah, that is because you see her only when I am present, and when for my sake she makes superhuman efforts to appear what she is not. I, however, have surprised her when she is alone, and then—but I must not keep you talking over my miserable fears, when I know that, previous to your departure, you have much to do ; so *au revoir*, old fellow, and may you have a good time in the jolly old city, which I suppose it will never be my lot to see again."

.   .   .   .

It was four o'clock when the two

friends bade each other good-bye, and
as Horace did not intend leaving
London till the evening train to Paris,
he had still some hours of leisure upon
his hands. The first of these he employed after a fashion which he had
for some days meditated, namely, in
paying a visit to Mrs Vavasour in
South Kensington. He had succeeded
in making Mr Vavasour's acquaintance,
and also in producing so favourable an
impression on Dolly's father, that he
was now, with that father's consent,
about—without, it must be owned, very
sanguine hopes of success—to put an
end to his uncertainties, and make to
the *volage*, laughter-loving Dolly an
offer of his hand and heart.

His intimacy with that young person
had of late greatly increased. It was
the avowed object of her father to

make but a short stay in London, the strained relations which existed between himself and his wife fully accounting, in the opinion of his friends, for the resolution he had formed. In furtherance with this object, he had purchased a large steam yacht, in which it was his intention to cruise during the remaining winter and the early spring months in the Mediterranean, and Dolly, who was a first-rate sailor, had indulged in the hope that she might be selected as her father's companion in the lengthened absence which he planned. In this, however, she was fated to be disappointed; a sea voyage and a complete change of scene had been ordered as the sole chance of restoring Lady Alston to health, and Hugh Vavasour had, in consequence, offered Alston and his wife berths on

board the *Camilla* for as long a period
as it suited them to remain on board.
The offer was by Charlie gratefully
accepted. His former prejudice against
Vavasour was entirely overcome, for the
latter, grey-haired and sorrow-stricken, was
clearly more an object for compassion
than for jealousy, and in fact Alston
was at present too entirely absorbed in
anxiety concerning his wife's health for
memories of the past, when she was
bright and blithesome as the day, to keep
any lengthened hold upon his thoughts.
Dolly, resting her hopes of accompanying
her father chiefly on the fact of which
she had long been cognisant, namely, that
he did not consider her mother a good
and efficient chaperon for a daughter so
young as she, was bitterly disappointed
when the intelligence reached her that
Ettie and Ettie's husband were chosen

instead of his own child, to be his companions in his wanderings. For the first
time in her life she felt jealous of this
sister, her near relationship to whom
she had been forbidden to claim, and
she kept repeating angrily to herself,—

"What is she, that he should prefer her
to his own child? She cannot care for
him as I do," and hot tears, as this thought
crossed her mind, rose to her long lashes, and
were still pendant there, for the girl felt too
spiritless to wipe them away, when, towards
the hour of five o'clock, the name of Mr
Horace Vane was announced by the "single
handed" man-servant, who alone Mrs Vavasour's limited income enabled her to keep.

The moment for putting into practice
Mr Vane's project was clearly not propi-
tious, but it was not his custom easily to
abandon a purpose formed, and therefore he
advanced with a bold front to the encounter.

CHAPTER XI.

DOLLY, who, on the young man's entrance, was seated on the music-stool, was the first to speak.

" Oh, Mr Vane ! " she exclaimed, lifting her tearful eyes to his, " have you heard what is going to happen ? The Alstons are going to sail with father in the *Camilla*, and I have so longed to go ! Is it not hard that I should be left at home ? "

Horace, who entertained an entirely private opinion that the reason why Dolly was not included in the yachting party arose from her father's wish that he (Vane) might, were she left in

England, succeed in winning her for his wife, felt slightly guilty as he listened to Dolly's complaints of her ill-usage.

"You do feel sorry for me, don't you?" she asked again, and she looked so pretty, with her glistening eyes still gazing wistfully into his, that it needed an effort on her lover's part to reply calmly to her question.

"Indeed I do," he, seating himself beside the music-stool, said; "but not more sorry than I should feel for *any* grief of yours. It is, the doctors say, so essential for Lady Alston's health that she should go on this trip."

"But why am I not to go as well?" Dolly broke in impetuously. "The yacht is very large, and surely I have a better claim than Lady Alston has to be with my father now. Can you tell me, Mr Vane, what his reasons are for leaving me behind ? "

" Perhaps," answered Horace evasively, "it was considered advisable to separate Lady Alston from all associations with the past. You were much with little Fay, you know, in former days."

" Not more than Sir Charles was, and if the reason you give is the right one, it seems to me that Lady Alston had better go in my father's yacht alone."

She had spoken without due reflection, and in another moment had regretted her hasty words, for Vane's look of surprised reproof distressed her much. She did not love him, she had often told herself, but she greatly valued his good opinion, and was in her heart ashamed of the jealousy of her half-sister which she had just evinced.

The girl's nature was a generous one, and her conscience having told her how grievously she had erred in even remembering the prejudices which on board the *Princess Carmen* she had imbibed, she hastened to retrieve her error.

"It was wrong of me to speak so," she said, "but if you knew me better you would not be surprised. I am a terribly impetuous party, and the bad habit of saying what I think has never yet been scolded out of me."

"You have yet to learn by experience the importance of the truth that words were given us to conceal our thoughts. Well, I am glad for my own sake that so it is, for I have a question to ask you, and I feel persuaded that you will at least give me a truthful answer. Will you be my wife?"

The demand was by Dolly so wholly unexpected, that for a few moments she was silent, her large eyes being fixed in amazement on Vane's anxious face ; at length she said,—

" I don't think you can really mean what you say ? "

" And why not ? " was his surprised response. " I have never yet said what I do not mean, and, in a matter so important as this, I am hardly likely to commence changing the habits of a life. What reason have you for supposing that I did not mean what I said ? "

Dolly's pretty cheeks grew crimson as she felt herself thus brought to book ; nevertheless, she answered the point-blank query bravely.

" Because of a conversation which I once overheard at a dance between you and another gentleman. It told me a great many things, and, amongst others, that I am not considered at all an eligible wife for a prudent man to choose."

Horace, seeming not the least abashed, smiled as he replied,—

"I remember the circumstance to which you allude. My companion was my brother Fred, a clergyman, as perhaps you know?"

"But not a very charitable one, for he seemed to think that my mother's daughter must necessarily be a bad girl."

"Hardly that; and, if you recollect rightly, one of the two, which was I, disputed the point with him altogether; and now, having as I hope, justified myself in your eyes, I ask you again. Will you be my wife? Do not keep me on tenter hooks. I have waited long and patiently, for, Dolly, little as you may have guessed the truth, I have loved you — well, ever since you were a tall, long - legged girl in short petticoats, with two thick plaits of hair falling down your shoulders."

" Oh," cried Dolly, laughing outright, " you could not have cared for me then ! I can see myself now, a dreadful creature with spindle shanks and long black stockings."

" Exactly, but I was clear - sighted enough to perceive potentialities which have been more than realised ; and were it only for my faith in the future, I deserve, I think, some little reward. Say, have you any love to give me in return ? "

" A little — yes — perhaps," the girl, still smiling, rejoined. " But not enough. If I married, I should like my love for my husband to be ' immense.' "

" And is there no chance," smiled Vane, " that your little love for me, may grow into something larger? Besides " (this more seriously), " what can a child like you know of *immense* love. Surely you have never yet felt it ? "

Again the hot blood of shame rushed to the girl's face and neck, but, true to her character for frank speaking, she answered in a low tone, but firmly,—

" If I have, it is over now, for I never wish to see the man I thought I loved again."

Had Horace Vane placed entire faith in the reality of this bygone passion, this confession on Dolly's part would probably have produced the effect of quelling the love fire that was burning in his breast, but there was that in the girl's outspoken fashion of confiding to him her past weakness, which, together with her youth and inexperience, inclined him to greatly doubt the reality of the love for another which she had just confessed ; and it was this doubt that induced him to say, in a half-jesting tone,—

" I hope that you exaggerate in your own mind the strength of your former feelings ; but it is, at any ⟩ rate, satisfactory to hear that you entertain such exalted notions of the love which a husband should inspire. The man would be indeed happy could he find himself the object of such devotion."

"Oh, now you are laughing at me," said Dolly, almost tearfully, "and what I said was really true. I should like to love my husband very much indeed — more than I love you now—"

"But do you not think that in time, and as I have now, as you say, no rival to contend with, that the love I long for will come? Dolly — my poor little thoughtless darling — you have much to learn —you have never really loved. Will you not let me teach you how great a joy it is to give yourself heart and soul to a husband who adores you?"

He had risen (even as she had done) as he spoke, and leaning his stalwart six feet of manhood against the piano, looked, as indeed he was, one whose love whispers were little likely to be breathed in vain even into ears which had already listened to the insidious voice of the tempter. Poor little Dolly, she had only, with her fresh, girlish lips, tasted of the cup which had been held to them, but having had that small experience of love's power, she did not see without visible emotion the signs of passion which gleamed in Horace Vane's dark eyes. Her girlish bosom rose and fell, and the deepening colour in her sweet young face betrayed the fact that she dared not meet the ardent gaze which she felt, rather than saw, was fixed upon it. He was very merciless. It was such luxury to watch the long quivering lashes as they swept over her blushing cheeks, that for a few moments he resisted the longing to throw his arm round her supple waist, and cover her ripe lips with kisses. For he felt that he had gained the day! Dolly was no ice maiden, and although it might be that his triumph was more over her senses than over her heart, yet Horace, experienced man of the world although he was, felt no fear for the future. The girl had had her lesson, and he had known and studied her long enough to be well assured that the "immense" love of which she had thoughtlessly spoken would yet be his.

"Have I conquered, darling?" he said at last; and then, before she was aware of his intention, his arms were round her, and her glossy head was resting, well content, upon his shoulder.

Were his the first kisses that a lover had ever pressed upon her lips? He feared to ask the question then, but the moment was not long in coming, when Dolly, whose love, as her sweetheart had fondly hoped, had grown with the growth of his, assured him of her own accord, and with the sweet, frank smile which he always found so irresistible, that, with the exception of her father's, no lips of mortal mould had even touched those which Horace Vane claimed now to be his own.

CHAPTER XII.

" Must you really go to Paris ? London will seem terribly dreary when the yacht has sailed, and when you also will have gone away. I wonder," asked Dolly saucily, " whether there is any real reason for your going ? "

The lovers are again *tête - à - tête,* but this time it is in Curzon Street that they are, as Charlie Alston phrased it, " enjoying their ante-nuptial honeymoon." Both he and Ettie, to say nothing of Mr Vavasour, are well pleased with Dolly's engagement, and that young person is now fully reconciled to the evil, as she at first considered it, of not being invited to join the party on board the *Camilla.* Horace Vane had, after his acceptance by Dolly, delayed for two days his departure for Paris, but the moment when he must put himself into the mail train, *en route* to that delightful city, is now fast approaching, and he is busily employed in stamping for the post the last letters previous to his departure.

Standing behind her lover, and half-tearfully watching his proceedings, is Dolly. Her appeal has been uttered very plaintively, and, a proof that it has not been made in vain, he says,—

" Is there any real reason, you ask, darling, for my going ? Well, in the first place there is this : 'Absence,' it is said 'makes the heart grow fonder,' and if you should perchance miss me, you may learn to love me better."

" How teazing you are ! " retorts Dolly.

" I asked you for a real reason, and you invent one in which there is not a single atom of sense. Now, please to tell me really and truly why you are going to Paris ? "

" Well, you inquisitive little woman, if you must know," and his arm steals round the girl's slender form as he prepares to do her bidding, " I have promised to look up a rather complicated legal case for a friend, and as I cannot say to him *yet*, ' I have married a wife, and therefore I cannot go,' I am bound to keep my promise."

" And how long shall you be away ? "

" That will depend upon the progress I make in my work. It may take me a week, or a fortnight, according to circumstances."

" And, in the meantime, I must stay with my mother, who is more difficult to live with than ever. She is constantly abusing father for not, now that he is so rich, giving her a larger income, and she says such dreadful things about him and dear Ettie, that I cannot bear to listen to her."

Horace Vane's brow grew dark as night as his *fiancée* thus poured forth her complaints.

" I wish to God," he said passionately, "that you were not forced to pass the time of my absence under Mrs Vavasour's roof."

" It is father's wish, you know," rejoined Dolly sadly. " He does not care for people to speak more disagreeably than is necessary about their separation."

" Tell me," exclaimed Vane abruptly, and speaking in a tone which startled Dolly, " whether or no your dislike to living under your mother's roof had anything to do with your acceptance of myself? You began by saying that you did not love me."

"And it was quite true, but I do love you dearly now, and the thought of living with my mother had nothing to do with—with what I did. You should not say such horrid things," and the ready tears welled up to the poor child's eyes as she wound up her pathetic reproach.

"Forgive me, sweet one, I was a fool," cried Horace, as he pressed her closely to his breast; "and do not punish me by thinking harshly of my jealous folly when I am far away. And now," looking at his watch, "I must be gone. *Au revoir*, my child, and write me nice long letters to the Hôtel Meurice to console me whilst I am away."

There was, in fact, no time to lose. A few passionate kisses are given and

returned, the hansom cab bearing Vane to
the station rolls along the silent street,
and Dolly Vavasour is left to her loneliness and tears.

.　　.　　.　　.　　.　　.　　.　　.

Horace Vane did not reply altogether
falsely when he assured his sweetheart
that legal business in behalf of a friend
summoned him to Paris. He had for
some time past been privately engaged
in following up a clue which he was not
without hope might eventually lead to
the discovery of the Alstons' child. He
entertained reasonable grounds for sus-
pecting that it was in Paris the little
one was secreted, and he therefore resolved
on proceeding thither, with the hope (on
which he abstained from enlarging whilst
conversing with his friends) of succeeding
in the endeavour to restore little Fay to
her sorrowing parents.

Taking up his quarters in Meurice's
Hotel, he, during several days after his
arrival, haunted the gardens of the Tuileries,
with the idea of finding, amongst the merry,
beautifully-dressed children who laughed
and played beneath the chestnut trees,
the golden-haired darling who had been so
cruelly parted from those whose cherished
jewel she was. His search proving fruit-
less, he reproached himself for his folly
in that he had imagined it probable that
little Fay's guardians, whose object was,
of course, to keep her whereabouts as
secret as possible, would permit of her appearance in the Tuileries gardens, where
at any moment she was, of course, liable
to be recognised by one or other of the
travelling English who, at all seasons of
the year, are either passing through, or
sojourning in Paris. The conviction of
his mistake produced a change of

tactics, and he took to making excursions into the environs of the city, keeping a watchful eye, meanwhile, on all those, the children more especially, by whom in his peregrinations his path was crossed. For several days he wandered and watched unsuccessfully, but just as he had begun to fear that his quest would prove abortive, the "unexpected," as is so often the case, happened, and the torch of hope was lighted anew in the bosom of Charlie Alston's friend.

On the second Sunday of his stay in Paris, he purchased a first - class ticket at the St Lazare station for Versailles. The carriage in which he happened to take his seat was, with the exception of himself, empty, but, it being one of those of which the *walls* of separation do not reach within twelve inches or so of the compartments' roofs, it soon became clear to him that the carriage in his immediate rear was fully occupied.

The train had scarcely done more than commence to slowly roll away from the station, when the voice of a Frenchwoman, loud and shrill, and speaking excitedly — a circumstance that caused her words to be distinctly audible above the rattle of the train, attracted his attention.

" *Ah, mon Dieu, petite,*" were the words he overheard, " *éloigne toi de la porte, et surtout ne joue pas avec le bouton Si la porte alloit s'ouvrir, tu tomberois sur la voie.*" *

* "My God, little one," it said, " keep away from the door, and above all, do not play with the handle. If the door were to open, you would be thrown out on the road."
" And I should be crushed : is it not so ? "
" Yes ; into a thousand pieces."
" But Jean Marie would mend me again, as he did my doll when it fell out of the window."

" *Et je servis écrasée : n'est ce pas ?* " responded a child's voice, which sent a thrill through the listener's frame.

" *Oui ; cassée en mille morceaux.* "

" *Mais Jean Marie me raccomodera, comme il a fait pour ma, pouppée quand elle est tombée par la fenêtre.* "

The laugh which followed this childish pleasantry reminded Horace so forcibly of that which in her happier days was wont to ripple so readily from the lips of Charlie Alston's wife, that he felt strongly tempted to take a surreptitious glance over the partition, in order to see the face as well as hear the voice of the last speaker ; but he wisely forbore. The case, as he was well aware, was one which, under the most favourable circumstances, would call for extreme caution, and he therefore wisely decided to wait till the stoppage of the Train—whether at Versailles or wheresoever his fellow-passengers might be journeying—in order to ascertain, as they left the carriage, what manner of child it was whose voice and laugh had so greatly excited his curiosity.

His suspense was not of long duration. The train stopped at Versailles, and there descended from it two well-dressed women and a little child—a child which, although more than a year had elapsed since he had seen it, he recognised, to his intense delight, as the one whose loss had embittered the once happy lives of its parents. There was the same golden hair, the delicately-tinted skin, and the joyous, bounding step of the lost little one, and Horace, as at a cautious distance he followed the trio to their destination, was greatly struck by the contrast between

the child's happy *insouciance* and the
look of saddened resignation which had
become a fixture on Lady Alston's still
lovely face. Truly, as he had once said
to Charlie, it is well for children that
their memories are short!

It was at a good-sized house, *entre
cour et jardin,** in the Rue des Reservoirs,
that the little party stopped, and, having
entered the porter's lodge, Vane judici-
ously contrived to ascertain from 'that garrulous individual the names of the lately
arrived ladies. They were *les* Demoiselles
Mauprat, and rented an apartment *un
troisieme.* The child was an orphan, of
whom *ces demoiselles* were the guardians.

Furnished with these particulars, Mr
Vane's next step was to inquire the
name and address of the most respectable
solicitor that in the town of Versailles

* Between court and garden.

was to be met with, and this information having been obtained, the Englishman lost no time in laying before Monsieur Ducrot every particular concerning the abduction, eighteen months previously, of the little girl in question.

"You can make oath, I conclude, as to the child's identity?" asked the lawyer. "Has she any particular mark by which you could recognise her? for I fear that a chance resemblance would not be sufficient to prove your case."

"The lost or stolen child had a small dark mole under her left ear," answered Vane.

"That is enough, monsieur. Now we have something solid to act upon," said the lawyer, and upon this assurance Vane departed, well pleased at the result of his visit.

CHAPTER XIII.

BEFORE Horace and the lawyer parted, it had been agreed between them that, on the following day, M. Ducrot should go alone to the Rue des Reservoirs, and, sending up his card to the Demoiselles Mauprat, should request the honour of an interview. The description given to him of the stolen child was sufficiently minute to enable him to decide whether or not the little one of whom *ces demoiselles* professed to be the guardians was in truth the one of whom the Englishman was in search.

"If the child answers your description, I will," he said to Vane, "join you in

the street. To betray any signs of suspicion to these ladies would, I think,
be a mistake. As the intention doubtless
is to make profit of the child, they
would be quite capable, were their fear
of detection to be aroused, of conceal-
ing the little one elsewhere."

Vane fully concurred in the lawyer's
view of the case, but the quarter of an
hour, for it was hardly more, of suspense
which he underwent during Monsieur
Ducrot's absence he found a very hard
one to endure. In his own mind, he
entertained hardly a doubt that his little
fellow-traveller of the previous day was
indeed his lost favourite; but then,
according to the lawyer, the identification
of the child depended almost solely on
the existence of the *grain** de beauté*
which the little one used playfully to

* *Anglice*, mole.

call her "black currant;" and in the course of eighteen months (Vane was profoundly ignorant in such matters) might not the mark have either become too faint to be discerned, or have disappeared from the delicate skin altogether?

The excitement under which the barrister was labouring proved so intense that, albeit by no means subject to nervous weakness, he found it a positive relief when Monsieur Ducrot, advancing towards him with a smile, was the first to speak.

"*Je vous félicite, monsieur,*" he commenced, "*ces demoiselles sont apparement des coquines de la premier ordre.** They received me, as I could perceive, with a certain embarrassment, which I endeavoured to allay by assuring them that my visit need not alarm them, and that I regretted

* "I congratulate you, sir, these ladies are apparently first-class rogues."

greatly the necessity of deranging them. But the fact was that I possessed an English client, who had been driven by the loss of his child into a state bordering on madness, and who, whenever he heard mention of a little girl of four or five years old, possessed of golden locks, would not be satisfied without making sure that it was not his own little Fay. I pronounced the word loudly, hoping to see in the little one some result of the sound, but, none appearing, I began to praise the child's beauty, especially that of her hair, which hung in a profusion of loose curls about her ears. I had by this time enticed it near me, for I have children of my own, and know how to deal with them, and whilst it was playing with the *bréloques* on my watch chain, I lifted a lock of her pretty hair, and there, sure enough, was the sign you spoke of—a dark *grain de beauté* under the left ear *de la charmante petite de-moiselle.*" *

"Thank God!" exclaimed Horace fer-vently, and in his excitement, and the instinctive craving of a tender heart for human sympathy, he stretched forth his hand to the lawyer. The latter, although probably taken aback by this impulsive act on the part of a phlegmatic English-man, did not prove unresponsive, and, after a cordial pressure of his new friend's muscular fingers, continued his narrative thus :—

"I, of course, made no allusion to the important discovery I had made, and after a few more civil speeches, took my leave. I left them, I am persuaded, without a suspicion on their part of the real object of my visit, and now all that remains is for us to apply to the Commissary of

* Of the charming little lady.

Police for an order to obtain possession of the child. He will, of course, accompany us to the Rue des Reservoirs, and I anticipate no difficulty in obliging these women to surrender the little one to its rightful guardian."

It would be a difficult task to do fitting justice by description to the happiness experienced by Horace Vane as, accompanied by the friendly lawyer, he bent his steps towards the official residence of the Commissary of Police. He figured to himself the rapture of the parents as they clasped their recovered treasure to their hearts, neither, as was only natural did the tide of joy rise less tumultuously, in his breast for the reason that it was to *his* exertions in their behalf that, under Providence, their happiness would be due.

On his arrival at the police office, Vane found that, before he could obtain the assistance of the Commissaire, he must not only repeat the particulars of the case as he had already imparted them to the lawyer, but must make good his right to claim, on Sir Charles Alston's account, the child for which he had so long been seeking. These preliminaries having been satisfactorily arranged, the Commissaire, duly accompanied by his deputy, drove off with the Englishman and Monsieur Ducrot to the apartment of the two middle - aged single ladies who, by the lawyer, had been unceremoniously denounced as *coquines;* and having climbed to the third story, demanded, after knocking loudly at the door, admission "in the name of the law."

It was twelve o'clock, and, on the entrance of the party, a trim maid-servant was clearing away the remains of the meal with which it is the habit

in France to supplement the matutinal
cup of chocolate or coffee. At the summons of the officers of the law, the
damsel gave a piercing shriek, whilst
ces demoiselles rose from their seats,
with terror visibly marked upon their
faces. They were still in morning *des-
habille*, and, with their grizzled heads
uncovered by caps, were not precisely
pleasant objects on which to look.
Little Fay, as we may now call her,
had been playing with her doll, but on
the entrance of the strangers she stood
still, and fixed her large blue eyes in-
quiringly upon Horace Vane. He, whilst
the Commissaire was explaining to the
jabbering women the cause of their
domiciliary visit, called suddenly in English to the child,—

"Come to me, little Fay; surely you
remember your old friend Ray Vane?"

Then a miracle was wrought, or rather some chord of memory was of a sudden struck, and the "chain of silence" which so long had held that infant mind imprisoned, was broken, for the intelligent little creature nestled closely to Horace Vane's outstretched arms, and, looking up fearlessly into his kind face, whispered, in the language which probably had been during many months unheard by her,—

"You not daddie!"

Then Vane, taking her in his arms, kissed her rosy lips, and told her, in French and in language suited to her tender years, that he was going to take her to her daddie, and to the mumsey who had grieved, and cried sorely for the little one she had lost. Fay, with widely-opened eyes, listens like one suddenly awakened in a strange bed from a dream, and who, wondering where she is, feels half afraid to question those about her as to her whereabouts. All is chaos for the moment in her mind. Memories of the days when she used to ride, a small triumphant queen, on the shoulders of the big slave whose voice is so unlike those of *ses tantes** (as she has been taught to call *ces demoiselles*), crowd around her, and greatly bewilder and daze her tender brain.

"Shall you like to travel with me in a big ship?" Vane, whose arm is encircling this lovely small *trouvaille*,† has just asked her, and she, reminded by the query of a striking event in her young life, is about to give her companion the benefit of her nautical experiences, when a harsh voice suddenly calling out "Adéle" arrests the words on her lips.

"*Dis—donc petite chipie*," shrieks the

---

* *Anglice,* her aunts.   † Discovered one.

elder Mademoiselle Mauprat, "have we not always been good to thee? Since thine aunt brought thee here, an orphan, to our cares, have we not fed and clothed thee as if thou wert our own?"

Fay answers this pathetic appeal by a quiet "*Si, mademoiselle*," but she makes no attempt to free herself from her new friend's embrace, and soon after, Vane, leaving the lawyer, who had received his previous instructions, to settle matters with *ces demoiselles*, carries away his prize in triumph.

His first act is to procure a respectable *bonne*, or nurse, for the little girl, and his next, a more difficult task by far, is to telegraph to the Alstons that he is about to pay a visit to the *Camilla*. He must be careful to say nothing in his despatch that is calculated to greatly agitate the delicate woman, who, albeit she has striven throughout her great sorrow to see the sunshine, which is "above us still," has been greatly shaken in health by the grief that would have its way. Nevertheless, the mere fact of his coming could not but have an all important significance in the eyes of both parents. He had read in *Galignani* that the *Camilla* was at Gibraltar, and he therefore, after much and anxious deliberation, telegraphed to Charlie as follows :—" Wish to see you. Shall be at Marseilles on 10th February. Wait my coming there."

This message having been despatched, Horace Vane, with a heart overflowing with gratitude to God, and satisfaction in his own success, engaged *coupé lits* for himself and his prattling charge, and started by express train to Marseilles.

CHAPTER XIV.

"OH, Charlie, what can it mean? Something gone wrong about Dolly, I fear!" exclaims Ettie, when she and her husband have, with beating hearts, inspected the telegram which the steward of the *Camilla* has brought on board.

"Probably," responds Charlie, who believes nothing of the kind; "and the poor old boy is taking a trip abroad to shake off the blue devils."

Lady Alston had not been deceived, although she had endeavoured to appear so, by the tone in which these few words were said, and on scanning Charlie's sunburnt face, she perceives that it has lost some of its bronzed, healthy hue.

"What is it, darling?" she says softly, laying her white hand upon his shoulder, whilst Hugh Vavasour, standing over against the weather bulwark, watches them both intently. "You do not believe what you are saying, and you are afraid—is not he, Mr Vavasour?—to tell me the truth."

"The truth is not to be spoken at all times," remarks Vavasour, with a strange laugh which has of late become so habitual to him that his guests have ceased to notice it. On the first occasion of her hearing it, Ettie had been not a little startled by the eerie sound, and had remarked upon its strangeness to her husband; he, however, had ridiculed her half-formed fears, telling her that to laugh in that sort was probably a peculiarity which, during his residence in the Argentine Republic, their host had contracted.

"Oh, Mr Vavasour!" exclaims Ettie,

"do not encourage him to hide what he thinks from me. I have not shown myself such a coward hitherto, have I, dear?" addressing Charlie, " that you should be afraid now to tell me that you believe this telegram has reference to our child."

She speaks so calmly, as well as looks so precisely her pale, normal self, that Alston feels convinced of the uselessness of any further attempt at concealment. Ettie, who is a sensible young woman, must be as well aware as he is himself, that few things are less likely to happen than a jilting of Horace by his sweetheart, and in the next, that, were so improbable an event to occur, Horace Vane would be little likely to travel express to Marseilles in order to personally announce the fact of his discomfiture. No ; the truth was patent to all, that Vane's telegram, guardedly though it was worded, had to do with Fay, and only with that long - lost child of their affections ; consequently, in the state of uncertainty as to the nature of the intelligence which they were so soon to learn, it behoved the deeply-agitated parents to bear, with what courage and patience they could summon to their aid, the suspense to which they were doomed to suffer.

Hugh Vavasour lost no time in giving orders to his sailing-master to get the yacht under weigh for Marseilles.

" I wish with all my heart," he said to Ettie, " that I could as easily command the removal from your breast of every burden. I wonder," he said musingly, as, seated on a folding-chair on deck, he stroked with his long thin fingers his grizzled moustache, " whether, had you been able to foresee this terrible sorrow, you would have—" and he stopped abruptly, afraid, it almost seemed, of having exceeded the bounds which his long friendship with Lady Alston in some degree authorised.

But she understood his half-finished question, and, greatly in the dark as she had ever been regarding the nature of his feelings towards her, she answered it with impulsive warmth.

" Whether I would have married Charlie, you would ask? Yes; and a thousand times, *Yes.* I have had my sorrows, but there has been a loving heart to share them with me, and if, after so much darkness, we are at last to see the silver lining behind the cloud, my joy, like my past griefs, will be felt and understood. The dear husband who has 'wept with me tear for tear, will not be wanting in heavenly sympathy with my joy.' "

In her turn she stops suddenly, startled and surprised by the expression of her companion's face, and then, laying a gentle hand on his arm, she says softly,—

" Oh, how unfeeling I have been to boast as I have been doing of my own happiness, when you are so sad and lonely. Dear Mr Vavasour, when I think of all that you have been to me, how you took me by the hand when I was utterly poor and friendless, the thought that but for me you need never have known the awful truth which has darkened your life fills me with remorse and sorrow."

" Hush ! It was dark long before that revelation, terrible as it was, came to me. How could I have long loved a woman capable of such vile, such barbarous deception ? I was taken by a pretty face—men are such arrant fools !—and never imagined that a woman who seemed so soft and gentle could be so hard and cruel."

" Do not think of her, dear friend," Ettie

says tenderly ; "you have your children, especially your little Dolly, to love, and then, am not I almost your child ? " (The swift shudder which, at this suggestion, passes through his frame, is happily unseen by Ettie, as she continues her well-meant attempts at consolation.) " It pains me, I own, to remember that I am my mother's daughter, but, being hers, I have almost a right, have I not, to call you father ? "

Greatly to her surprise, Vavasour makes no reply in words to this kindly question, but with a repetition, faint, yet still audible, of his strange laugh, moves slowly towards the fore part of the vessel. When, after a few minutes, he returns, he says quite calmly,—

" We shall soon fetch Marseilles," then, struck by the rapidly increasing pallor of her lovely face, he quickly adds, " Forgive me, I forgot. Vane ought either to have said more or less. You are very brave, and it is not for me to aggravate your sufferings."

For a moment or two she cannot speak, for the knowledge that her suspense is drawing to a close is causing her breath to come short and quickly. She is conscious that the yacht, which had been dashing at high pressure rate through the quietly slumbering waters, is slackening speed, and a sudden fear seizes her, that if little Fay has at last been found, she, the mother, who so long had sought her sorrowing, may not live to press her darling in her arms, and this fear gives her strength to whisper,—

" Send Charlie to me," a request which, whilst her companion hastens to obey, elicits a groan, and another of his sinister laughs from Vavasour.

" Do not leave me, darling," the weak woman murmurs, and above the unavoidable clamour which always accompanies the shortening of sail and letting go the anchor, the sweet, tremulous voice is plainly heard.

" I won't, my poor darling," Charlie says, as he takes the place vacated by Vavasour beside her, " but, for my sake, be brave. Here, doctor," this to the *Camilla's* surgeon, a kindly, sympathising young man, who, foreseeing that his aid may be required, has advanced towards Lady Alston's chair, " see what you can do with this unreasonable passenger," and he was again moving away, his own agitation being almost uncontrollable, when Ettie's reiterated cry of, " Oh, do not leave me, Charlie," brought him back to his young wife's side.

For a moment there is comparative silence. The anchor has been dropped, and the schooner, with her sails furled, lies motionless upon the waters of the Mediterranean Sea. Then, of a sudden, a voice from the shore sings out lustily,

"*Camilla*, ahoy," and the slender hand which Alston holds imprisoned in his own trembles alarmingly in his grasp. There is but little further delay. Suspense will soon be exchanged for certainty, for a boat has been quickly manned, and in a few more minutes Horace Vane, springing through the gangway, stands on the *Camilla's* deck.

He sees at a glance that there is no time to lose, and therefore says at once, as he presses Ettie's clay-cold hand,—

"She is here—at the hotel—and safe and well."

But Ettie scarcely heard the words. She has fainted dead away, whilst the doctor, kneeling beside her, is busied in restoring animation to the mother's pallid form.

"Will she live, doctor?" Charlie, in hoarse accents, asks.

"Oh, yes, Sir Charles," was the smiling reply, "joy does not kill."

And truly enough, as if in corroboration of his assertion, Lady Alston at that moment opens her eyes, her husband's relief at the welcome sight plainly demonstrating to him that a joy, however great, purchased by the sacrifice of her life would have been deprived of half its value. Before she fainted, Ettie had realised the blessed truth that had fallen from their friend's lips, and was now, with "rapture wild," silently thanking God for the great mercy that he had vouchsafed unto her.

"Will she know us?" asked Charlie. "Oh, I trust she has not quite forgotten her childhood days."

"She is gradually recollecting everything," answers Vane, and then, at a whisper from Alston, he descends through the gangway to the boat that is in waiting for him.

He has gone to fetch little Fay, and restore her to her parents' arms.

.   .   .   .

Over the meeting we must draw a veil. It was only by slow degrees that the child fully recognised the truth that she was once more with the dear parents from whom she had been so rudely torn. Then recollection of the days which had followed on her abduction was confused and slight, but those whose eyes were gladdened by her joyous presence were too happy in watching the development of her infant memory to grudge the time of waiting. They looked upon the restoration of their darling as a boon given by Heaven, which made ample amends for the sufferings of the past, so true is it that,—

> " Sorrow touched by God grows bright
> With more than rapture's ray,
> As darkness shows us worlds of light
> We never saw by day."

CONCLUSION.

HIS HEART WAS HOT AND RESTLESS.

It has clearly not been the intention of an all-wise Providence that humam beings should enjoy lives of perfect happiness here below, and Charlie Alston and his wife, in the midst of their recovered joy, and apparently in the possession of every blessing that life can bestow, were nevertheless doomed to undergo the irritation of the proverbial crumpled rose-leaf, of which a far-seeing disposer of events is, we are led to suppose, the originator.

What the nature of that crumpled rose-leaf is, the following dialogue between the husband and wife will doubtless make clear.

Ettie is seated under the shelter of the weather bulwarks upon the *Camilla's* deck, with her small daughter leaning against her skirt, and listening with rapt attention to the pretty tale, of which maternal love is the inspirer, as it flows *so* eloquently from the mother's loving lips.

"And did the kind gentleman find little Tom?" asks Fay, in her pretty broken English, but she does not wait for an answer, inasmuch as "daddie's" head has made its appearance above the companion hatch, and with a shout of joy the ungrateful little puss flies towards him in the hope —one not destined to be disappointed—of enjoying a ride, by no means at foot's pace, along the snow-white decks, perched on the strong shoulder of her paternal parent.

"Quicker, daddie, quicker; Fay, want spur for gee-gee," cries the little one, as she mercilessly, and "with a will," applies the stimulus of her dainty little kid slipper to the broad chest of her willing slave.

"There, you small unfeeling tyrant," pants Charlie, as he lifts Fay from her coign of vantage, and replaces her by her mother's side ; " rather hot work," he added, wiping his steaming forehead, "with the thermometer more than ninety in the shade," and then, seated on the companion hatch, he contemplates, infinitely to his satisfaction, the beauty of both mother and child, as, costumed in Redfern's prettiest yachting dresses — the one an abridged edition of the other—they smile at him beneath the friendly shelter of the awning.

"We must not spoil her, must we ?" Ettie is saying, as she fondly strokes the golden head of her "first and fairest," "and happily here is Elise come to carry her off to sleep. *Dors bien, mon ange*," she says, as Fay, rushing impetuously into her mother's arms, narrowly escapes toppling over that still delicate mother, together with herself and the folding-chair in one disastrous heap; after which happily averted accident, peace reigns for awhile upon the *Camilla's* snow-white decks.

They are proceeding under very easy sail, for, unless absolutely necessary, Vavasour objects to the use of steam, towards Genoa. It is a six knots an hour breeze, no more, which is carrying them onward, and Ettie, who is impatient to find herself in the City of Palaces, chafes a little at the delay.

"Would you prefer a white squall from the west?" asks her husband chaffingly. "You have only to name your wishes to Vavasour. *Si c'est possible cele fait, c'est impossible cela se fera.*"*

"I know. He is kindness itself. He always has been so very good to me."

"Too good, I used to think," said

* If possible it *is* done, if impossible it *will* be done.

Charlie, who has drawn a yachting chair
next to hers, and has fixed his eyes on the
lovely face to which recovered happiness
has lent again some of its sweet carnation
hue.

" Too good ? " she repeats questioningly.
" I do not understand."

" I was fool enough once," says Charlie,
" to imagine that his affection for you was
not wholly disinterested, but I have recovered from that *accès* of folly now.   I did
him a gross injustice—at least, what I may
call perhaps a sort of an injustice, seeing
that we are not always answerable for our
thoughts and wishes ; but however that may
be, there has been something lately in Vavasour's manner that has puzzled me not a
little.   I have consulted Townley about him,
and he agrees with me that the man has
greatly changed of late.   Have you not remarked it, darling ?   I am afraid, from what

Townley tells me that he does not sleep at night."

Ettie has laid down her work—a tiny silken sock which she is knitting for Fay —and has clearly given up her entire thoughts to the subject which her husband has introduced.

" I have noticed," she says, after a pause, "that he is altered. He takes no notice now, as he used to do, of Fay ; and then his laugh—oh, Charlie ! it is so extraordinary. Hardly a human sound. What is it, do you think ? " she asks, in a low voice, and anxiously, " that can have changed him so ? "

" Well, poor fellow, if you come to that, he has had troubles enough to account for any amount of sleeplessness. A proud, reserved man—think what that terrible discovery must have cost him. I never like to think or talk of Mrs Vavasour as your mother, Ettie, and I have sometimes fancied

that the knowledge that she is your mother
has distressed and pained him."

" It is sad to think," said Ettie mourn-
fully, that the fact of being my mother's
daughter should create a prejudice against
me."

" I said nothing about a prejudice, dearest,"
rejoined Charlie; " you mistook me altogether
—so much so that now I feel compelled to
tell you that I used to fear that—that—er,
his kindness, as you call it—towards you
was due to quite a contrary feeling."

" But, dear," said Ettie in amazement,
" he was a married man ! "

" True, I forgot that," with a little well-
pleased inward laugh at his wife's *neuf*
ignorance—Music Hall singer although she
had been—of the world and its ways.
" But whatever the cause of his present
depression may arise from, we must endeavour, when we get him on shore at

Genoa, to make him take an interest in the old palaces, and the pictures. He is fond of Art, and if we can make him feel that there are still things in life worth living for, he might shake off the memories which have lately, I fear, been gaining upon him."

On that evening, the last before the Port of Genoa would be sighted, it was remarked with much satisfaction by Hugh Vavasour's guests that he had appeared during dinner, and even later in the evening, to have in a great measure recovered his usual spirits. He spoke cheerfully of his daughters, and especially of Dolly, and of the satisfaction which her engagement to Horace Vane afforded him. Also, a symptom which Lady Alston hailed as highly favourable, he insisted on Fay making her appearance at dessert.

" Then you have decided not to prosecute that infamous Frenchwoman ? " he asked of

Charlie, whose attention was at that moment fully occupied by the apparent intention of his small daughter to choke herself with the stone of a preserved greengage. " Guilt such as hers should not go unpunished."

" Ettie has an idea," answered Sir Charles,—" is it not so dear ?—that she can best show her gratitude to God by bestowing pardon on the injurer."

" It is like her," rejoined Vavasour, looking earnestly at the sweet face beside him, " to forgive the author, or the instigator, whomsoever it may have been, of all her sufferings."

" You always had a far better opinion of me than I deserve," smiled Ettie ; " perhaps," added she, as she held out her hand, preparatory to bidding him good-night, " mine is only a precautionary measure. What has happened "— this with a nervous shudder—" may happen again."

"God forbid!" ejaculated Vavasour, whose eyes followed, with a kind of dazed expression, her graceful form, till the cabin door closed behind his guests, and he was left, save for the presence of the doctor, alone.

For a few minutes he remains silent, and with his arms folded on the table, then he suddenly rouses himself from his reverie, and says,—

"Doctor, I want you to feel my pulse, and tell me whether you consider my state of mind to be such that I can be trusted to make what may be called a rational will. I have drawn up mine to-day, not being one of those fools who imagine that, because they make preparations for Death, it is likely to be, in consequence, an hour nearer to their elbows; but, as my dispositions might some day be disputed, your testimony as to my state of mind would, in that case, be of

value. I must ask you and Captain Wilder
to witness my signature, only, as you would
be both," smiling, "under other circumstances very slightly benefited by the document, I will ask you to accept instead, free
of legacy duty, this token of my regard,"
placing in the doctor's hand a cheque for
one hundred pounds as he spoke. "Do not
thank me. I have more money than I
know what to do with ; and have the kindness to send Wilder here."

It requires but a few minutes to bring
the sailing-master, a retired captain of an
East Indiaman, to the saloon, and then
Hugh Vavasour, soon after pressing on the
weather-beaten old salt a similar "proof of
friendship" to that which he had bestowed
upon the doctor, proceeds in a low but firm
voice to read aloud the short document
which contains his final wishes. In it there
is no mention whatever either of his wife

or of Sir Charles, but, after bequeathing thirty thousand pounds to each of his daughters, and a year's pay to each of the *Camilla's* crew, he leaves the whole of his fortune, amounting to half a million sterling, to Henrietta, Lady Alston, "as a proof of the testator's esteem and affection."

"And now, doctor," said Hugh, baring his wrist, "if you will kindly ascertain whether, as far as you can judge, I am of sane mind, I will sign my name, which you and the captain will be good enough to witness."

Mr Townley had been much struck by a remark made by Mr Vavasour during dinner, and knowing himself to be rather a privileged person with his employer, he ventured, as he laid a light finger on the latter's pulse, to say,—

"Miss Fay will be more in danger of abduction than ever now; but, sir, may I be allowed to ask whether you have any idea that the crime you spoke of did not originate with the Frenchwoman?"

For all reply Vavasour said, as he dismissed his two witnesses for the night,—

" Report travels fast and far in these days, and even so far as Buenos Ayres I learnt— Well, gentlemen, what I knew full well before—that another such woman is not to be found upon the earth as the lady who has honoured us with her company to-night."

" I wonder," whispered the doctor to his companion, as they reached the cabin of the latter, " what and how much he knows. There is some mystery in this, and it is singular his not having named Sir Charles in that Will of his."

" Is it?" rejoined the unsuspicious old sea-dog, as he carefully locked away his unexpected *douceur* and mixed for himself a three-water grog by way of a sleeping draught. "Anyway, he's a first-rate chap to sign articles under."

And having so said, the worthy sailor, having ascertained that all was "snug" on board for the night, "turned in," and doubtless slept, as he deserved to do, the sleep of the just. No presentiment of coming evil disturbed his slumbers, and therefore his astonishment may be more easily imagined than described when, with his bronzed and bearded face colourless with alarm, the yacht-steward entered his cabin at eight bells on the following morning with the news, tremulously delivered, that on board the vessel, Mr Vavasour was nowhere to be found! After a minute search from stem to stern, for the missing man, had been effected, the only conclusion to be arrived at was that he had met his death by drowning, but on questioning the sailors, only one bearded tar could

throw the faintest light upon what might, in
the moonless night, have taken place. The
men whose watch it was, had apparently
gathered in a group under the weather bulwark, and, with the exception of one melancholy howl from the captain's Newfoundland
dog, had heard no sound to break the still-
ness of the night. One man, and one alone,
who in his hammock had been dreaming
(probably, of the girl he left behind him),
declared that about midnight he had heard
a *splash*. But little credit was, however,
given to him for his superior knowledge.
We can all of us bear witness to the strange
jumble of fancy and reality in the stuff of
which dreams are made, and it is probable
that, whilst "Jack" was figuring to himself
the absent Sall wringing at the wash-tub the
soap-suds from her sousy arms, the falling
into the water of the self-doomed man
mingled with his love-sick visions, and for a

passing moment aroused him from his heavy slumbers.

And what, as he leant over the vessel's side and contemplated the water, bright with phosphoric light, into which he was about to plunge, could have been the thoughts of the man who, in the full vigour of manhood, had made up his sinful mind to take that awful plunge? High above his head the deep purple canopy of Heaven was studded with stars innumerable. " Jewels of pure gold," they twinkled with their myriad eyes upon the miserable mortal who, in sheer weariness of life, was about to rush, " unhouseled, unanointed and unanealed," into the presence of his Maker! Vavasour was a weak rather than a wicked man, and yet he never faltered in the purpose which had led him to the yacht's side that night. He had striven, and striven in vain, to endure with equanimity the sight of Charlie

Alston's happiness with the woman whom
he himself, still, to his heavy misfortune, so
fondly worshipped, and sooner than continue
to endure the jealous pangs which tore his
heart in twain, he, regardless of the sorrow
which his death would cause, rushed to
" the phantom of grisly bone" as a panacea
for his ills.

But albeit he was thus selfishly absorbed,
the last thoughts which occupied that
dazed and bewildered mind, as he
cautiously left the bulwark, and slid
noiselessly down by the vessel's chains to
the phosphorescent water, were of the
beautiful girl for whose love he had so
ardently longed, and whose loss had
driven him to despair and death. Silently
and surely the bright waves closed over
his guilty head, his only requiem being,
as I before said, a prolonged wail from
Neptune, the captain's dog, who might—

for dog's instincts are often keener than human reasonings—have received some secret warning that on that night another human soul had winged its melancholy flight away. It was truly a most sad ending to a nobly intended but mistaken life. In his ripe manhood, Hugh Vavasour had for the first time given the precious gift of his heart into a young girl's keeping, and to the last she had been unconscious of the boon. The knowledge that so it was had driven him at last to madness and to suicide. So true it is that—

> "Young man's love blazeth and is done,
> Old man's love burneth to the bone."

To Ettie, the intelligence that her old friend had, as there was too much reason to fear, met his death by his own hand, proved a terrible shock.

"Oh, Charlie, he could not have been himself," she moaned, "or else his end was due, perhaps, to accident. Only yesterday evening he seemed quite well and bright."

"And afterwards he signed his Will, leaving the bulk of his large property to you."

"Oh, I *am* sorry!" ejaculated Ettie.

"And so am I. It seems awful to profit by the poor fellow's death." And then Alston, remembering the overpowering causes of grief and shame which might have driven the unhappy man to suicide, would almost rejoice that his mental sufferings were over, and that, "after life's fitful fever" was ended, he, it might be hoped, "slept well."

There came a time when Ettie, who for a while refused to be comforted, could in some measure share in Charlie's satisfaction that her kind friend's days of suffering were at an end. The suspected cause of his death was, however, to her a source of lasting sorrow. The thoughts from which, when she had believed in her darling's death, had brought her comfort, were in this case of no avail, and when imagination—as it is always too ready to do—pictured to her a lifeless body lying, a hideous thing, deprived of Christian burial, fathoms deep beneath the sea, it needed all her belief in a pardoning God, and the certainty of a blissful resurrection, to recall to her mind the consoling truth, that those sad remnants of mortality were naught save,

> " A worn-out fetter that the soul
> Had broken and thrown away."

THE END.

COLSTON AND COMPANY, PRINTERS, EDINBURGH.

.